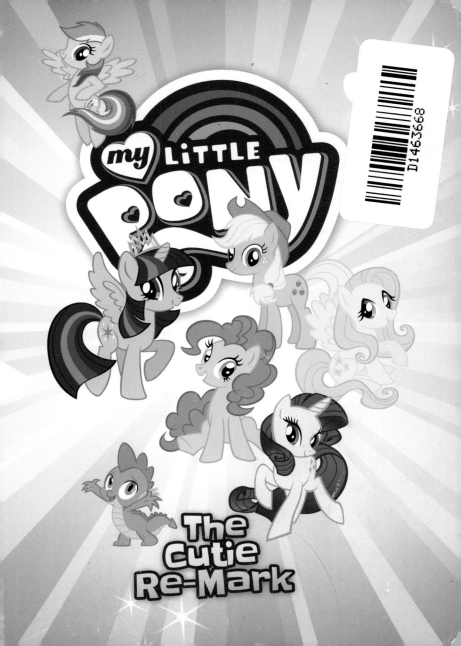

my LiTTLE PONY

The Cutie Re-Mark

Special thanks to Meghan McCarthy,
Eliza Hart, Ed Lane, Beth Artale,
Heather Hopkins, and Michael Kelly.

ISBN: 978-1-68405-306-3
21 20 19 18   1 2 3 4

Greg Goldstein, President & Publisher
Robbie Robbins, EVP & Sr. Art Director
Matthew Ruzicka, CPA, Chief Financial Officer
David Hedgecock, Associate Publisher
Laurie Windrow, Sr. VP of Sales & Marketing
Lorelei Bunjes, VP of Digital Services
Jerry Bennington, VP of New Product Development
Eric Moss, Sr. Director, Licensing & Business Development

Ted Adams, Founder & CEO of IDW Media Holdings

Licensed By:

www.IDWPUBLISHING.com

my LITTLE PONY
The Cutie Re-Mark

Story by
Josh Haber

Adaptation by
Justin Eisinger

Edits by
Alonzo Simon

Lettering and Design by
Gilberto Lazcano

Production Assistance by
Amauri Osorio

MEET THE PONIES

Twilight Sparkle

TWILIGHT SPARKLE TRIES TO FIND THE ANSWER TO EVERY QUESTION! WHETHER STUDYING A BOOK OR SPENDING TIME WITH PONY FRIENDS, SHE ALWAYS LEARNS SOMETHING NEW!

Spike

SPIKE IS TWILIGHT SPARKLE'S BEST FRIEND AND NUMBER ONE ASSISTANT. HIS FIRE BREATH CAN DELIVER SCROLLS DIRECTLY TO PRINCESS CELESTIA!

Applejack

APPLEJACK IS HONEST, FRIENDLY, AND SWEET TO THE CORE! SHE LOVES TO BE OUTSIDE, AND HER PONY FRIENDS KNOW THEY CAN ALWAYS COUNT ON HER.

Fluttershy

FLUTTERSHY IS A KIND
AND GENTLE PONY WITH
A BIG HEART. SHE LIKES
TO TAKE CARE OF OTHERS,
ESPECIALLY HER LITTLE
ANIMAL FRIENDS.

Rarity

RARITY KNOWS HOW
TO ADD SPARKLE TO
ANY OUTFIT! SHE LOVES
TO GIVE HER PONY
FRIENDS ADVICE ON THE
LATEST PONY FASHIONS
AND HAIRSTYLES.

Pinkie Pie

PINKIE PIE KEEPS HER
PONY FRIENDS LAUGHING
AND SMILING ALL DAY!
CHEERFUL AND PLAYFUL,
SHE ALWAYS LOOKS ON
THE BRIGHT SIDE.

Rainbow Dash

RAINBOW DASH LOVES TO
FLY AS FAST AS SHE CAN!
SHE IS ALWAYS READY TO
PLAY A GAME, GO ON AN
ADVENTURE, OR HELP OUT
ONE OF HER PONY FRIENDS.

Princess Celestia

PRINCESS CELESTIA IS
A MAGICAL AND BEAUTIFUL
PONY WHO RULES THE LAND
OF EQUESTRIA. ALL OF THE
PONIES IN PONYVILLE LOOK
UP TO HER!

The
Cutie
Re-Mark

IF SOMEPONY HAD TOLD ME WHEN I WAS A BLANK-FLANK THAT ONE DAY...

...I'D GIVE A SPEECH TO A CLASS AT CELESTIA'S *SCHOOL OF MAGIC,* I WOULDN'T HAVE BELIEVED IT.

BUT—

TWILIGHT PAUSES TO SHUFFLE HER NOTE CARDS.

VVRRRRNNN

I HOPE THAT I HAVE BEEN UP TO THE TASK, BECAUSE I CAN TELL THAT ALL OF YOU ARE...

...AND THAT THE FUTURE OF EQUESTRIAN MAGIC IS IN GOOD HOOVES.

CLAP CLAP CLAP

CLAP CLAP CLAP

WOW, TWILIGHT, THAT WAS EVEN BETTER—

CLAP CLAP CLAP

—THAN THE FIRST *ELEVEN* TIMES!

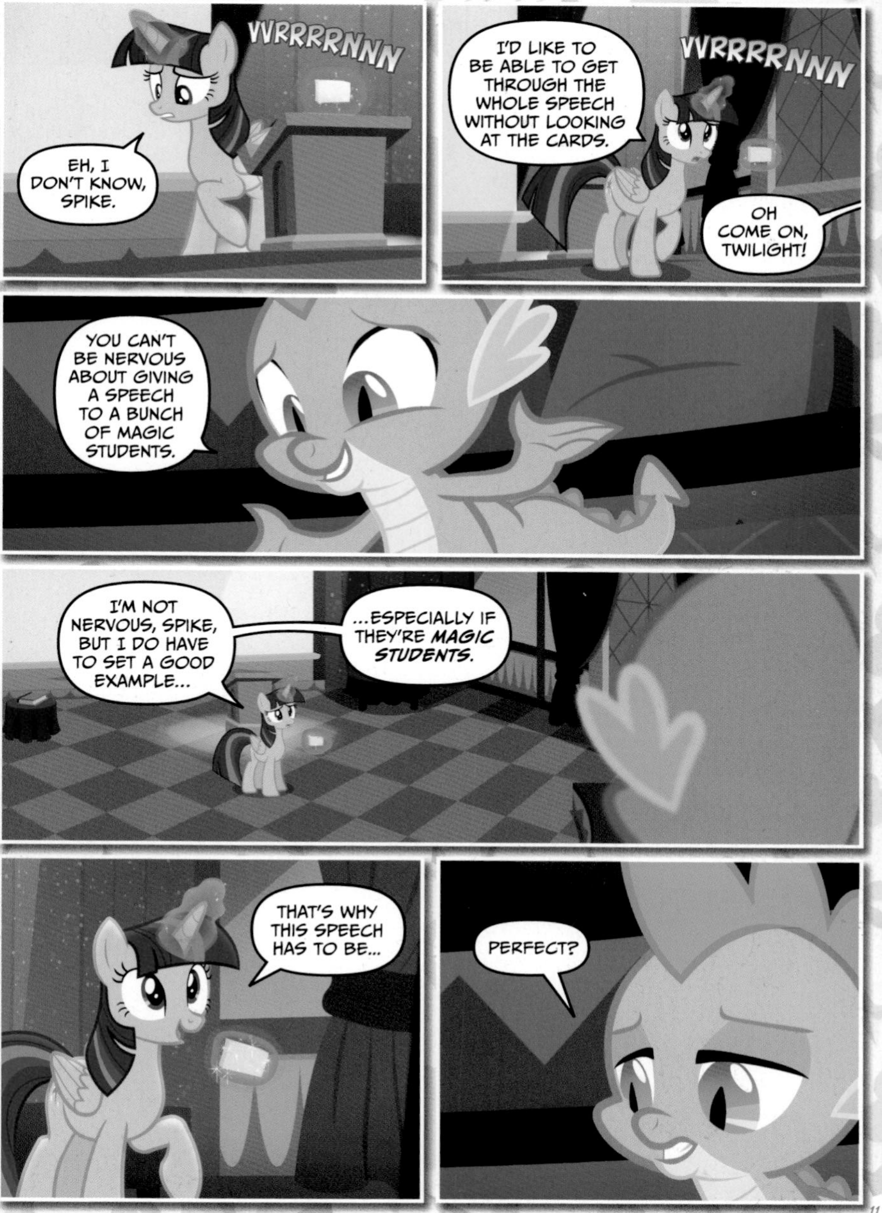
VVRRRRNNN
EH, I DON'T KNOW, SPIKE.
VVRRRRNNN
I'D LIKE TO BE ABLE TO GET THROUGH THE WHOLE SPEECH WITHOUT LOOKING AT THE CARDS.
OH COME ON, TWILIGHT!
YOU CAN'T BE NERVOUS ABOUT GIVING A SPEECH TO A BUNCH OF MAGIC STUDENTS.
I'M NOT NERVOUS, SPIKE, BUT I DO HAVE TO SET A GOOD EXAMPLE...
...ESPECIALLY IF THEY'RE *MAGIC STUDENTS*.
THAT'S WHY THIS SPEECH HAS TO BE...
PERFECT?

EXACTLY.

LET'S GO THROUGH IT ONE MORE TIME.

HUMPF

WHEN PRINCESS CELESTIA ASKED ME TO SPEAK TO YOU TODAY...

OH BROTHER...

OBVIOUSLY THE LONG-TERM EFFECTS...

...OF THE SIMULTANEOUS ACQUISITION OF CUTIE MARKS HAS YET TO BE DETERMINED, BUT...

AHEM. NEXT SLIDE, PLEASE.

UMMM, NEXT SLIDE?!

13

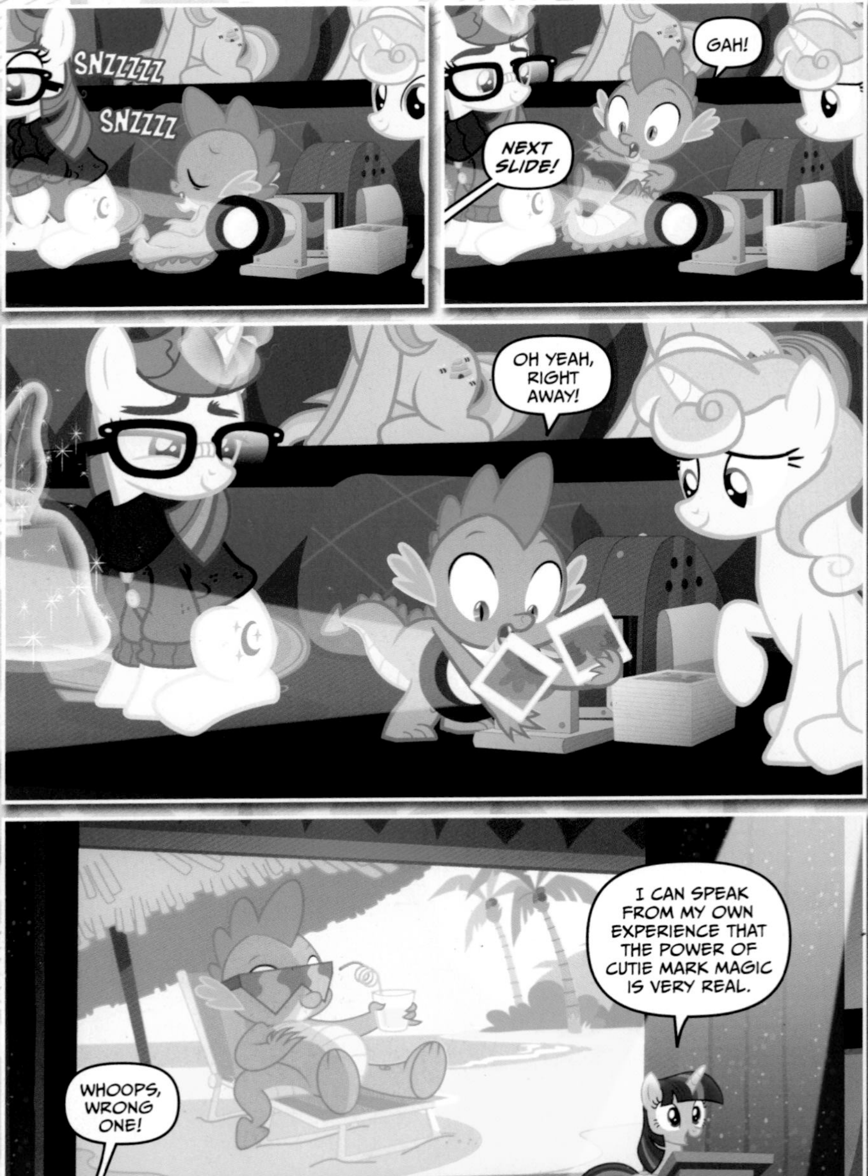
SNZZZZZZ
SNZZZZ
GAH!
NEXT SLIDE!
OH YEAH, RIGHT AWAY!
I CAN SPEAK FROM MY OWN EXPERIENCE THAT THE POWER OF CUTIE MARK MAGIC IS VERY REAL.
WHOOPS, WRONG ONE!

AND IN THE INSTANCE OF MY FRIENDS AND I, IT CAN BE TRACED TO A SINGLE EVENT.

FLUTTERSHY MIGHT NEVER HAVE LANDED IN EVERFREE FOREST...

WITHOUT RAINBOW DASH'S RACE TO DEFEND FLUTTERSHY'S HONOR, HER *RAINBOOM* WOULDN'T HAVE HAPPENED...

APPLEJACK MIGHT NEVER HAVE REALIZED THAT SHE BELONGED ON HER FARM...

IT MIGHT BE HARD TO IMAGINE, RARITY WITHOUT HER SENSE OF FABULOUSNESS...

AND PINKIE MIGHT NEVER HAVE DECIDED TO LEAVE HER FAMILY'S LAND.

TEE-HEE TEE-HEE

GIGGLE

BUT IT'S EVEN HARDER TO FATHOM WHAT MY LIFE WOULD BE LIKE.

WITHOUT THIS RAINBOOM, I MIGHT NOT HAVE GOTTEN INTO MAGIC SCHOOL.

CELESTIA WOULDN'T HAVE TAKEN ME ON AS HER PUPIL.

OR SENT ME TO *PONYVILLE* TO MEET MY FRIENDS.

TWILIGHT SCANS THE AUDIENCE AS SHE SPEAKS...

AND THE MOST POWERFUL THING ABOUT *CUTIE MARK MAGIC* THAT I'VE FOUND IS THE CONNECTION I SHARE WITH THEM.

WAIT, WAS THAT?!

COULD IT BE?

WAS THAT STARLIGHT GLIMMER?!

WHERE'D SHE GO?!

..BUT, UM...

WVRRRNNN

THE REAL QUESTION ABOUT CUTIE MARK... MAGIC... IS WHO IT SEEMS TO AFFECT...

BACK IN PONYVILLE...

WOOOOOSH

STARLIGHT GLIMMER?

I WAS SURE I SAW HER, SPIKE.

BUT WHEN I LOOKED AGAIN SHE WAS GONE.

I'M JUST WORRIED WHAT SHE COULD BE UP TO.

NOTHING GOOD, I BET.

I HEARD SHE WASN'T VERY HAPPY THE LAST TIME YOU SAW HER.

FORCING *EVERYPONY* IN HER VILLAGE TO HAVE THE SAME CUTIE MARK WASN'T RIGHT.

WE HAD TO DO SOMETHING.

AND NOW SHE'S COME BACK FOR *REVENGE*...

THE MENTION OF *REVENGE* STOPS TWILIGHT IN HER TRACKS!

OR SHE WAS JUST REALLY INTERESTED IN YOUR SPEECH.

HONESTLY, SPIKE, I'M NOT REALLY SURE *WHAT* I SAW.

BUT AS LONG AS I HAVE MY FRIENDS I KNOW EVERYTHING WILL BE ALRIGHT.

TWILIGHT AND SPIKE REACH THE PALACE...

MAYBE I WAS JUST MORE STRESSED ABOUT THAT SPEECH THAN I THOUGHT.

THAT SOUNDS BETTER THAN STARLIGHT GLIMMER COMING BACK WITH AN EVIL PLOT FOR REVENGE.

WELL, WHEN YOU SAY IT LIKE THAT, IT DOES SOUND KIND OF SILLY.

WHUMP

OR IT'S TOTALLY TRUE!

WELCOME HOME...

...TWILIGHT!

ZZZRRRTTTT

ZPP

STARLIGHT LEVITATES THE SCROLL HIGH IN THE CHAMBER...

ZZZZRRRRTTT

ZORT

OH NO!

WHAT ARE YOU DOING, STARLIGHT?!

HA HA HA!

I'D TELL YOU, BUT I DON'T WANT TO *RUIN* THE *SURPRISE!*

KRUNCH

GUESS I WON'T BE NEEDING *THAT* ANYMORE.

FWIP

YOU CAN'T STOP ME!

ZZZRRRTTTT

STOP HER, TWILIGHT!

VORT

BUT HER BLAST IS DEFLECTED!

NRT

AND A MIGHTY WIND BLOWS THROUGH THE THRONE ROOM...

SWOOOSH

...AS A STRANGE PORTAL APPEARS ABOVE!

KRRZZZKKKKK

SWOOOOOOOSH

ZZZRRRTTTTT

ZZZRRRTTTTT

ZORT

AND AS SUDDENLY AS IT APPEARED, THE PORTAL IS GONE!

VIPP

WHERE'D SHE GO?

I DON'T KNOW, SPIKE.

BUT I THINK WE BETTER FIND OUT.

I GUESS WE COULD START WITH THIS.

SPIKE, NO!

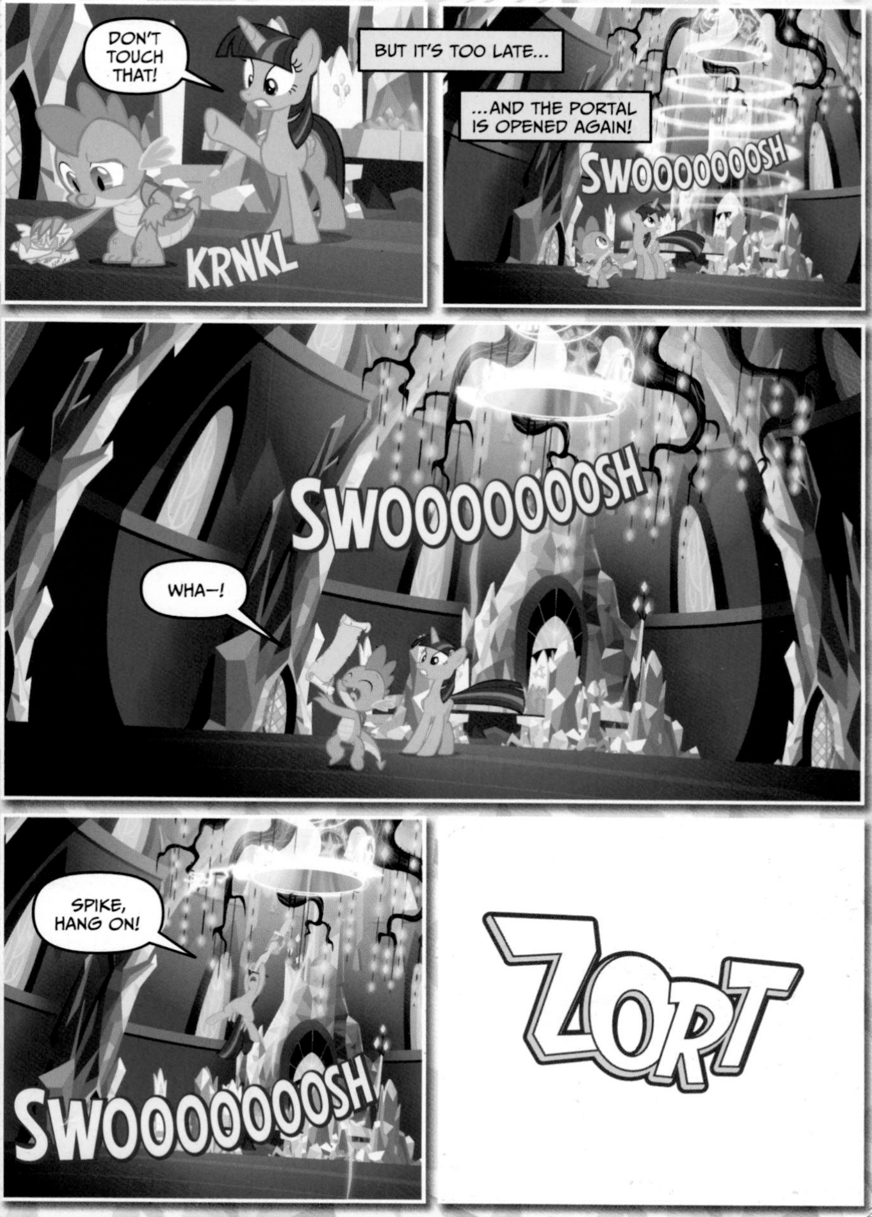
DON'T TOUCH THAT!
KRNKL
BUT IT'S TOO LATE...
...AND THE PORTAL IS OPENED AGAIN!
SWOOOOOOOSH
SWOOOOOOOOSH
WHA–!
SPIKE, HANG ON!
SWOOOOOOOOSH
ZORT

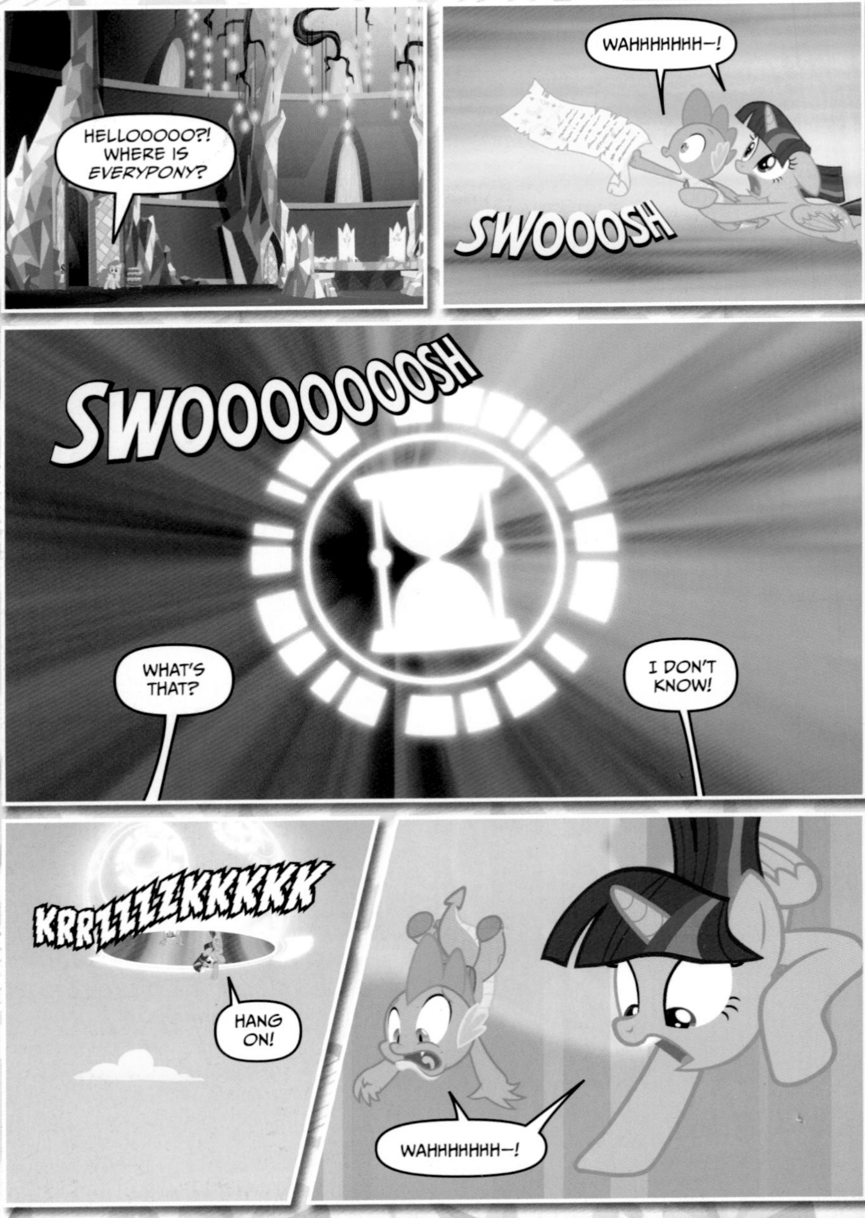
HELLOOOOO?! WHERE IS EVERYPONY?
WAHHHHHHH—!
SWOOOSH
SWOOOOOOOSH
WHAT'S THAT?
I DON'T KNOW!
KRRZZZZZKKKKK
HANG ON!
WAHHHHHHH—!

THAT'S WHEN TWILIGHT REMEMBERS HER WINGS.

NOOOOOO!

FLUMP

I CAN'T LOOK!

VVVRRRRNNNN

OH!

THANKS, TWILIGHT!

TWILIGHT USES HER MAGIC TO KEEP HIM SAFE.

WHERE ARE WE?

I'M NOT SURE...

CLOUDSDALE!

STARLIGHT DOESN'T EVEN HAVE WINGS.

WHY WOULD SHE COME HERE?

I DON'T KNOW, SPIKE, BUT IT LOOKED LIKE SHE COULD FLY WITH JUST MAGIC.

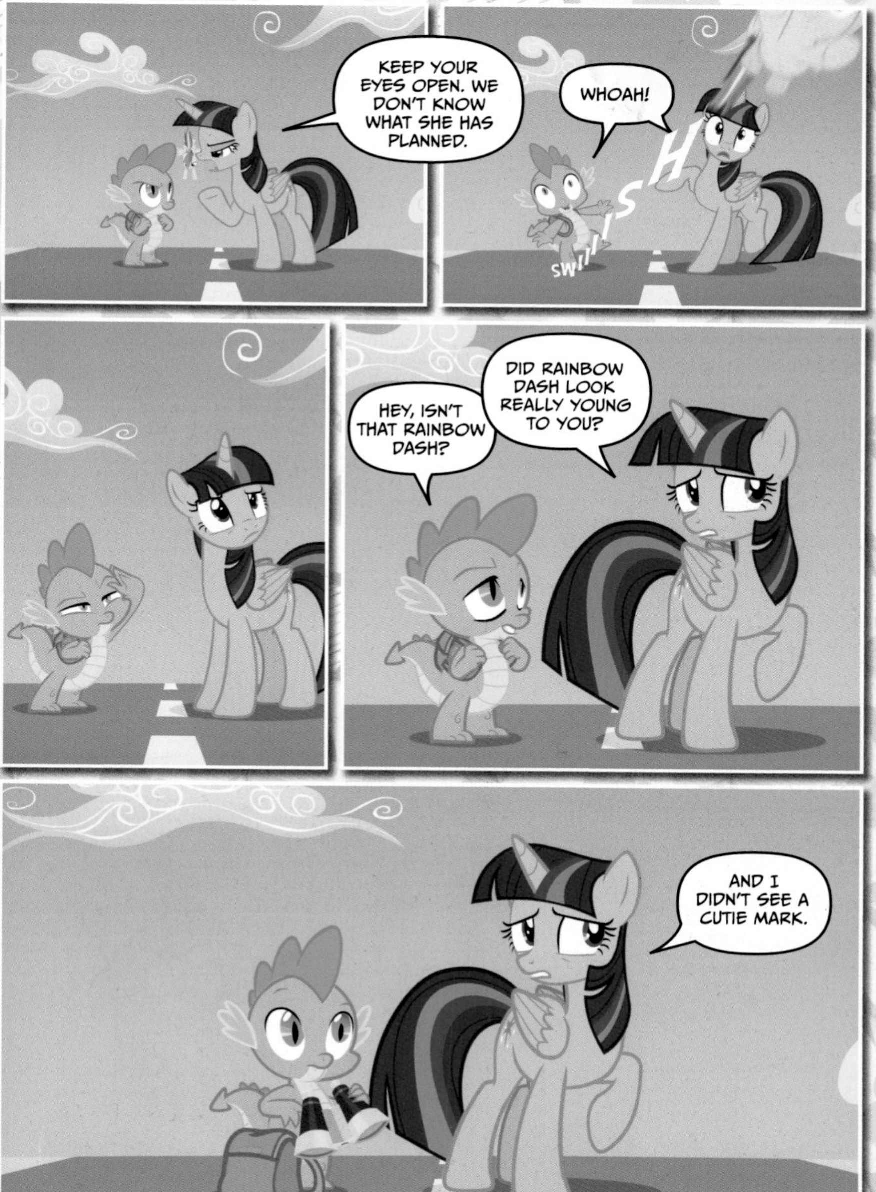
KEEP YOUR EYES OPEN. WE DON'T KNOW WHAT SHE HAS PLANNED.
WHOAH!
SWIIIISSH
HEY, ISN'T THAT RAINBOW DASH?
DID RAINBOW DASH LOOK REALLY YOUNG TO YOU?
AND I DIDN'T SEE A CUTIE MARK.

YOU DON'T THINK...

WE *TRAVELLED BACK IN TIME* TO WHEN RAINBOW DASH RACED THE BULLIES—

—WHO MADE FUN OF FLUTTERSHY AND PERFORMED HER FIRST SONIC *RAINBOOM?*

TRAVELLED BACK IN TIME? SPIKE, ONLY *STARSWIRL THE BEARDED* COULD DO SOMETHING LIKE THAT.

AND EVEN HIS SPELL JUST WENT BACK A WEEK.

HOW COULD STARLIGHT DO MORE THAN THE GREATEST WIZARD IN EQUESTRIA?

HMMMM...

WITH THIS.

OH, NO.

COME ON LET'S GO!

GO WHERE?

TO WATCH THE RACE! I DON'T WANT TO MISS THE *RAINBOOM.*

33

NEARBY, THE RACE IS ABOUT TO START!

START

FLUTTERSHY WAVES THE CHECKERED FLAG AND THEY'RE OFF!

FWOOOOOOOSH

THEN GETS MORE THAN SHE BARGAINED FOR!

WHOOOOAH!

FWIPPPP

TWILIGHT IS ABOUT TO LEAP INTO ACTION...

AAAAHHHHHH—

WAIT!

WE CAN'T CHANGE ANYTHING!

TAKE IT EASY, SPIKE. WE ALREADY KNOW HOW IT ENDS.

THAT DOESN'T MAKE IT ANY LESS EXCITING!

LOOK AT HER GO!

FWOOOOOOSH

YOU THINK YOU CAN BEAT ME?

WHAM

CHIRP CHIRP

OH YEAH!

WHUMP

SORRY, RAINBOW CRASH!

HEY!

FFWWWWWWWWWW OOOOOOOSH

SORRY ABOUT *THIS*.

XXXXRRTTTT

FFWWWWWWWWWWWWWWWWWW OOOOOOOOOOSH

JUST AS RAINBOW DASH IS ABOUT TO CREATE A *RAINBOOM*...

...STARLIGHT HITS HER WITH MAGIC!

ZZZRRRTTTT

WHICH STOPS RAINBOW DASH IN HER TRACKS!

HEY?!

WHAT GIVES?

HOORAY! HOOPS WINS!

WOOOOOSH

WHILE ELSEWHERE...

OH, HELLO.

...THINGS ARE QUICKLY CHANGING...

GOODBYE...

APPLEJACK, VISITING *MANEHATTAN*, DOESN'T GET THE *SIGN* SHE NEEDS.

FWWSSSSS

HMPF!

OUT ON PINKIE PIE'S FAMILY FARM...

...IT'S JUST ANOTHER DAY OF HARD WORK.

BETTER GET BACK AT IT.

RARITY SEES JUST ANOTHER ROCK...

NO BIG DEAL.

...THAT'S NOT SO IMPRESSIVE.

FWIP

EVEN YOUNG TWILIGHT
IS NO EXCEPTION...

HNNNNNGGG–

...UNABLE TO COMPLETE
HER FINAL PROJECT.

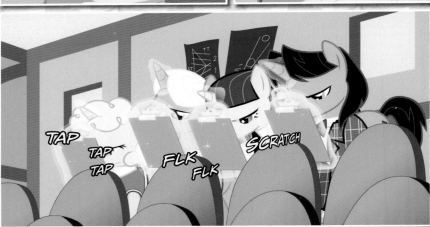

TAP

TAP
TAP

FLK
FLK

SCRATCH

WHAT'S GOING ON?!

BACK IN CLOUDSDALE...

UMMM...

WHAT DID YOU DO?

YOU ARE ABOUT TO FIND OUT.

VOOOOOSH

ANOTHER PORTAL!

UM, TWILIGHT...?

VOOOOOSH

XXXRRRTTTT

41

XXXXXRRRRTTTTT

AAAHHHHHH—

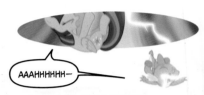

AAAHHHHHH—

WHAMMM

UNNNGH...

I DON'T KNOW WHAT STARLIGHT'S UP TO YET...

OW!

...BUT WE BETTER FIGURE IT OUT BEFORE IT'S TOO LATE.

UM... TWILIGHT...

I THINK IT ALREADY IS.

GASP!!

TWILIGHT, WHERE'S YOUR CASTLE?

43

THE MAP PULLED US BACK, BUT WHATEVER STARLIGHT DID IN THE PAST CHANGED THINGS HERE.

WE KNOW WHAT SHE DID. SHE STOPPED THE RAINBOOM.

BUT WHY? AND HOW DID WE GET HERE? AND *WHERE'S HERE?*

JUST THEN A MAGIC SCROLL APPEARS...

MORE LIKE *WHEN!*

VVRRRRNNN

WHAT DO YOU MEAN?

STARLIGHT ALTERED STARSWIRL'S SPELL...

...THEN SOMEHOW USED IT ON THE MAP TO TRAVEL INTO THE PAST AND CHANGE SOMETHING.

ONCE SHE DID, THE MAP PULLED US BACK TO THE PRESENT.

SO WE'RE BACK *WHERE*... I MEAN, *WHEN* WE STARTED?

NOT EXACTLY.

EVERYTHING'S DIFFERENT.

LOOK.

THE MAP DOESN'T EVEN MAKE SENSE ANYMORE.

THE CRYSTAL EMPIRE TAKES UP HALF OF EQUESTRIA.

PLUS THERE'S THE WHOLE MISSING CASTLE THING.

RIGHT.

THIS IS TOO BIG TO HANDLE ON OUR OWN.

YOU THINK?!

WE NEED TO FIND OUR FRIENDS AND GET HELP.

A WHILE LATER...

...THE PAIR APPROACH *PONYVILLE.*

IT LOOKS DESERTED!

THERE'S SOMEPONY.

WIP
WIP

BUT *SOMEPONY* LOOKS WORRIED!

AH!

FLUMP

I'M GETTING A BAD FEELING ABOUT THIS, TWILIGHT.

I KNOW, SPIKE. BUT THIS IS PONYVILLE. HOW BAD CAN THINGS BE?

IS THAT SUGAR CUBE CORNER?

I DON'T UNDERSTAND.

GAH!

HUFF HUFF

BANG BANG BANG

RARITY?!

RARITY?!

I DON'T THINK SHE'S HERE, SPIKE.

SNIFF!

I'M NOT SURE ANYTHING WE KNOW IS THE SAME...

BUT I KNOW ONE PLACE THAT COULD NEVER CHANGE.

A FEW MOMENTS LATER...

...BUT THINGS *HAVE* CHANGED!

WHAAAAA–?!

UH–?

TWILIGHT WALKS TO THE FACTORY AND WIPES THE DIRTY GLASS...

ERRRRRRP

MAYBE I CAN SEE SOMETHING...

A MACHINE IS MAKING THE APPLE SAUCE.

HHHHSSSSSSSS

CHUG CHUG

AND THERE'S APPLEJACK!

PSSSSSSSSH

CLANG

I WONDER WHAT HAPPENED?

WE NEED TO FIND OUT.

RMMMBBBLLL

APPLEJACK?

IT'S SO GOOD TO SEE YOU!

WHAT CAN I DO FOR YA?

WE COULDN'T FIND PINKIE OR RARITY OR FLUTTERSHY OR RAINBOW DASH...

AS TWILIGHT EXPLAINS, APPLEJACK GOES ABOUT HER BUSINESS.

...BUT I JUST KNEW *YOU'D* STILL BE HERE.

OF COURSE I AM...

THIS IS MY HOME.

BUT WHO IN TARNATION IS *PINKIE BOW* AND *FLUTTER DASH*?

OR YOU FOR THAT MATTER?

YOU DON'T KNOW WHO I AM?

NOPE. HONESTLY, THE ONLY NAME I RECOGNIZED IS *RARITY*...

...BUT SHE LEFT FOR *MANEHATTAN* YEARS AGO.

PROBABLY TO BECOME A WORLD FAMOUS FASHION DESIGNER, I BET.

NOT THAT I KNOW OF.

LAST I HEARD SHE WENT TO HELP WITH THE *CAUSE* LIKE *EVERYPONY* ELSE.

THE CAUSE?

THE WAR AGAINST KING SOMBRA AND THE CRYSTAL EMPIRE?

WHAT?!

WHERE HAVE YOU TWO BEEN?

ACTUALLY, IT'S *WHEN*.

I KNOW THIS IS HARD TO BELIEVE...

...BUT YOU AND I AND THOSE OTHER PONIES I MENTIONED ARE *FRIENDS*.

DID YOU BUMP YOUR HEAD ON A CRATE OF CIDER?

I'M TELLING YOU THE TRUTH AND IF YOU COME WITH ME, I'LL PROVE IT.

VVRRRRNNN

BUT TWILIGHT ISN'T LEAVING THE CHOICE UP FOR DEBATE!

WELL, I'LL ADMIT...

...I'VE LIVED IN THESE HERE PARTS MY *WHOLE LIFE* AND I'VE *NEVER* SEEN THIS BEFORE.

THERE'S ALSO SUPPOSED TO BE A CASTLE THAT GOES WITH IT.

BUT I STILL DON'T SEE WHAT IT HAS TO DO WITH YOU AND I BEING FRIENDS.

ANOTHER PONY NAMED STARLIGHT GLIMMER USED THIS MAP...

...TO TRAVEL THROUGH TIME AND CHANGE THINGS IN THE PAST.

CHANGE THINGS *HOW?*

WELL, FOR ONE THING, WHERE WE CAME FROM THERE'S NO *WAR WITH KING SOMBRA.*

THE NEWS CASTS A SILENCE OVER APPLEJACK.

MAYBE YOU COULD TELL US HOW THE WAR STARTED?

THEN WE CAN FIGURE OUT WHEN EVERYTHING CHANGED.

THAT'S EASY ENOUGH.

WHEN THE CRYSTAL EMPIRE RETURNED...

"...IT BROUGHT KING SOMBRA BACK WITH IT..."

"AND IT DIDN'T TAKE LONG FOR HIM TO FORCE EVERY ONE OF HIS SUBJECTS...

"...TO FIGHT FOR HIM AGAINST EQUESTRIA."

WE MUST STAND AGAINST THIS INJUSTICE!

CHARGE

ATTACK

"AND EVEN WITH PRINCESS CELESTIA LEADING THE CHARGE..."

HEH HA HA HAAA

"IT STILL TAKES EVERY LAST PONY IN EQUESTRIA...

BZZZZZZ

"...DOING THEIR PART..."

PHEW!

"...WORKING DAY AND NIGHT TO KEEP UP THE FIGHT."

NEXT STOP, FRONT LINES!

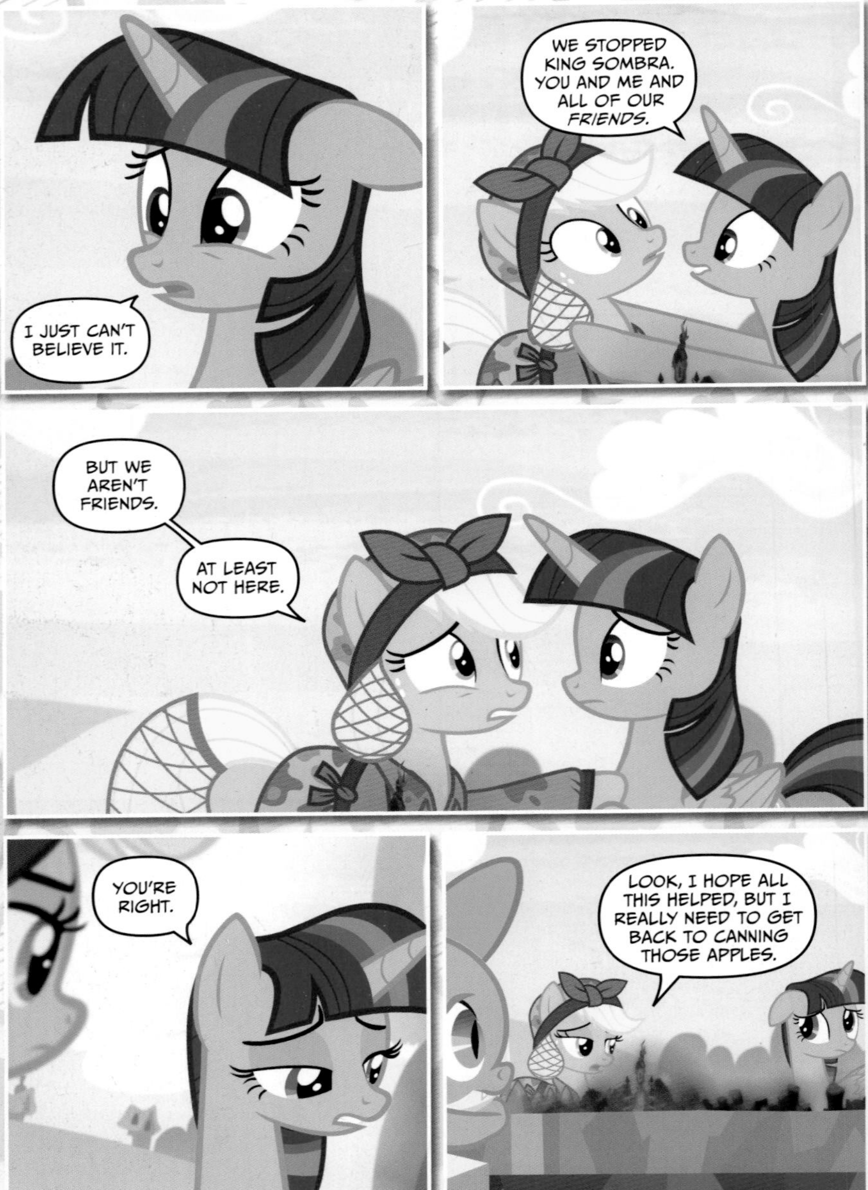

I JUST CAN'T BELIEVE IT.
WE STOPPED KING SOMBRA. YOU AND ME AND ALL OF OUR *FRIENDS.*
BUT WE AREN'T FRIENDS.
AT LEAST NOT HERE.
YOU'RE RIGHT.
LOOK, I HOPE ALL THIS HELPED, BUT I REALLY NEED TO GET BACK TO CANNING THOSE APPLES.

WE'RE GOING TO SET THINGS RIGHT.

I HOPE YOU DO.

SO... HOW ARE WE GOING TO SET THINGS RIGHT?

I DON'T KNOW!

THUD

THE ONLY THING WE KNOW FOR SURE IS THAT STARLIGHT STOPPED THE RAINBOOM.

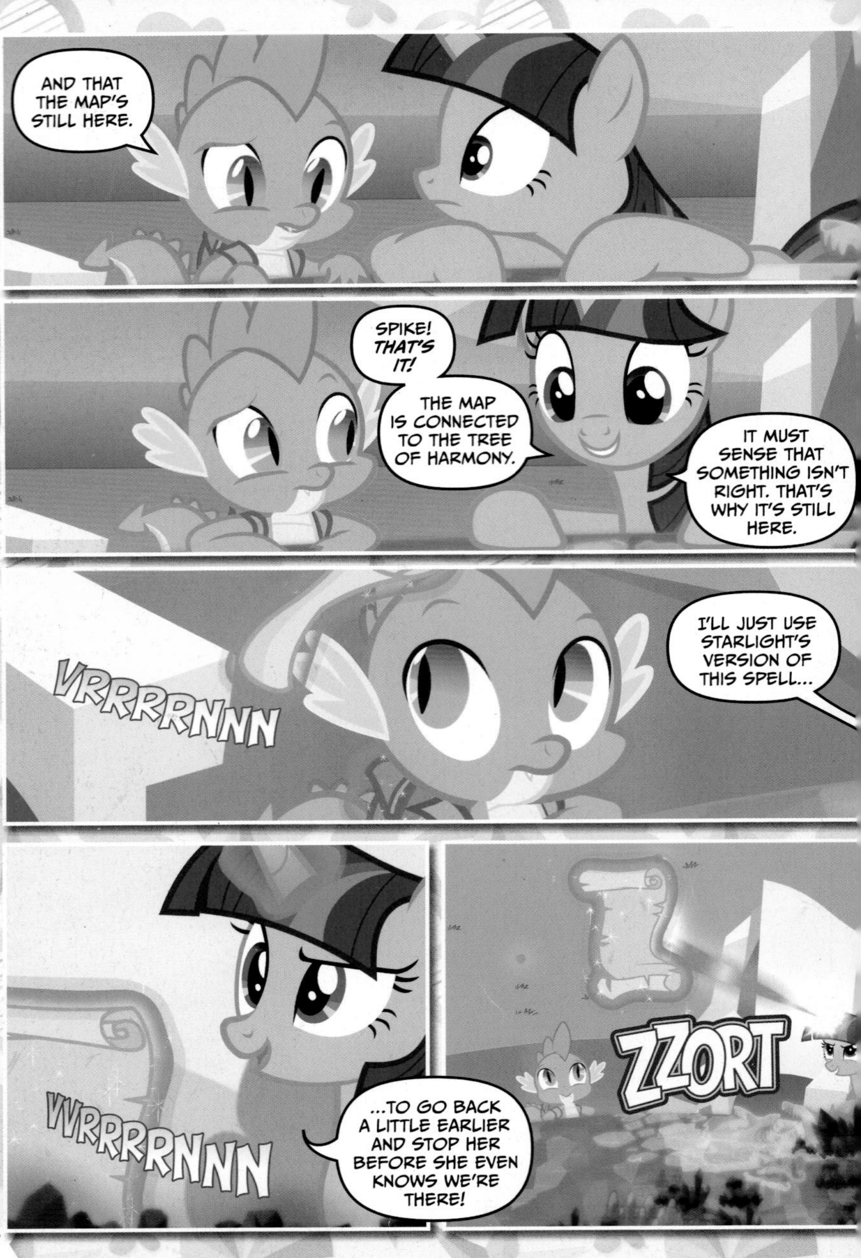
AND THAT THE MAP'S STILL HERE.
SPIKE! *THAT'S IT!*
THE MAP IS CONNECTED TO THE TREE OF HARMONY.
IT MUST SENSE THAT SOMETHING ISN'T RIGHT. THAT'S WHY IT'S STILL HERE.
VRRRRRNNN
I'LL JUST USE STARLIGHT'S VERSION OF THIS SPELL...
VVRRRRRNNN
...TO GO BACK A LITTLE EARLIER AND STOP HER BEFORE SHE EVEN KNOWS WE'RE THERE!
ZZORT

TWILIGHT'S MAGIC ACTIVATES THE PORTAL...

VVVVRRRRRNNNNN

...SENDING THEM TO *CLOUDSDALE!*

VVRRRRNNN

AHHH—

AHHHHHHHH—

THANKS!

WVUMP

ALL WE HAVE TO DO NOW IS FIND STARLIGHT AND—

ZAPP

THEY'RE TRAPPED!

WELL, *FINDING* HER WILL BE EASY.

THUMP

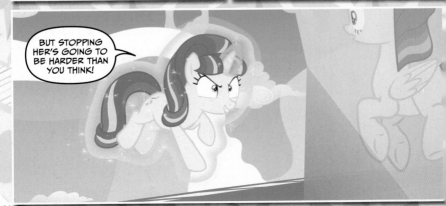

BUT STOPPING HER'S GOING TO BE HARDER THAN YOU THINK!

SORRY TO DISAPPOINT YOU...

...BUT I CREATED THAT SPELL TO SEND *MYSELF* BACK IN TIME.

SO EVEN WHEN *YOU* CAST IT—

—*I* STILL GET SENT BACK IN TIME.

IT WASN'T HARD TO CHANGE STARSWIRL'S SPELL.

HE'D ALREADY DONE THE HARD PART.

BUT FIGURING OUT I COULD USE THE MAP TO GO TO ANY TIME OR PLACE *AND* PULL YOU ALONG WITH ME?!

I EVEN IMPRESSED *MYSELF* WITH THAT.

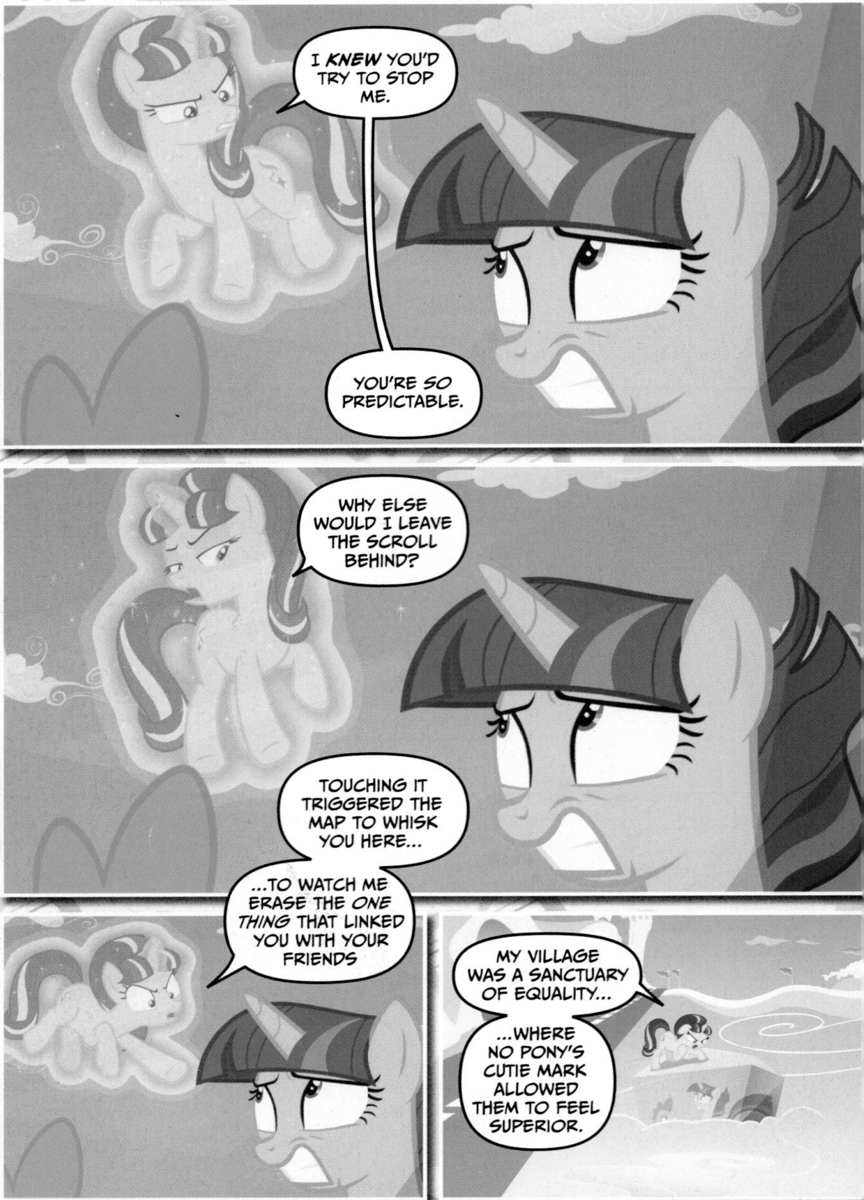
I KNEW YOU'D TRY TO STOP ME.
YOU'RE SO PREDICTABLE.
WHY ELSE WOULD I LEAVE THE SCROLL BEHIND?
TOUCHING IT TRIGGERED THE MAP TO WHISK YOU HERE...
...TO WATCH ME ERASE THE ONE THING THAT LINKED YOU WITH YOUR FRIENDS
MY VILLAGE WAS A SANCTUARY OF EQUALITY...
...WHERE NO PONY'S CUTIE MARK ALLOWED THEM TO FEEL SUPERIOR.

IT WAS A SPECIAL PLACE...

...AND THEN *YOU* AND *YOUR* FRIENDS TOOK IT *AWAY.*

NOW IT'S MY TURN TO TAKE SOMETHING SPECIAL FROM YOU.

WITHOUT THE RAINBOOM—

—YOU AND YOUR FRIENDS WILL NEVER FORM YOUR SPECIAL CUTIE MARK BOND.

CUTIE MARKS FOR CUTIE MARKS.

SOUNDS LIKE A FAIR TRADE TO ME.

TH WAK

FWIPPPP

EEEOOOOOOSHHH

EEEEAAAAAA—

VVRRRRNNN

VRRRRT

SMASH

I THOUGHT SO. HMPF.

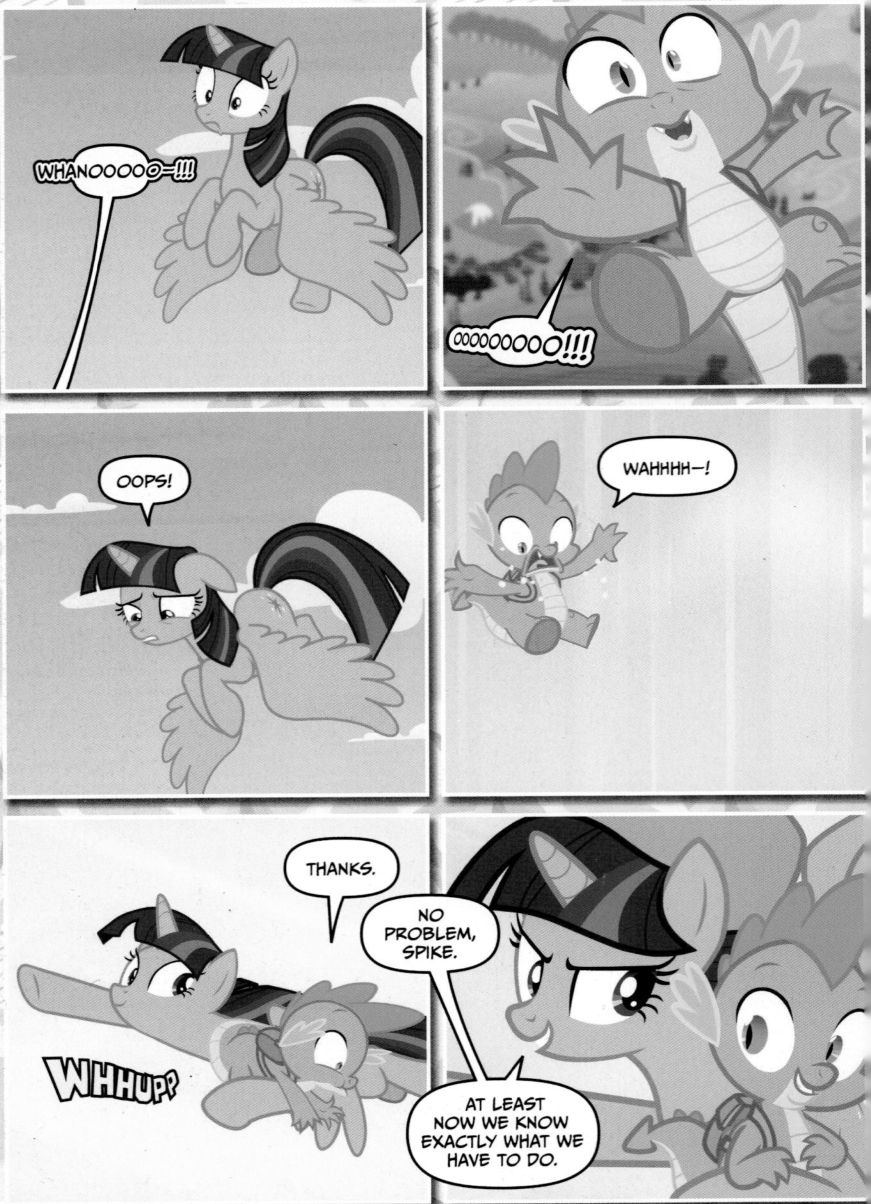

WHANOOOOO—!!!
OOOOOOOOO!!!
OOPS!
WAHHHH—!
THANKS.
WHHUPP
NO PROBLEM, SPIKE.
AT LEAST NOW WE KNOW EXACTLY WHAT WE HAVE TO DO.

A SHORT WHILE LATER...

...TWILIGHT AND SPIKE ARE LOOKING FOR STARLIGHT GLIMMER.

AND TRYING TO KEEP A LOW PROFILE.

OKAY. KEEP YOUR EYES PEELED.

WE HAVE TO STOP STARLIGHT...

...AS SOON AS RAINBOW DASH AND THOSE BULLIES RACE BY.

UM, TWILIGHT...

BE READY. BECAUSE SHE COULD POP UP ANYWHERE.

TAP TAP

LIKE OVER THERE?

WRRRRNNN

GAH!

JUST REMEMBER HOW YOU'D FEEL IF SOMEONE SAID THOSE THINGS TO YOU!

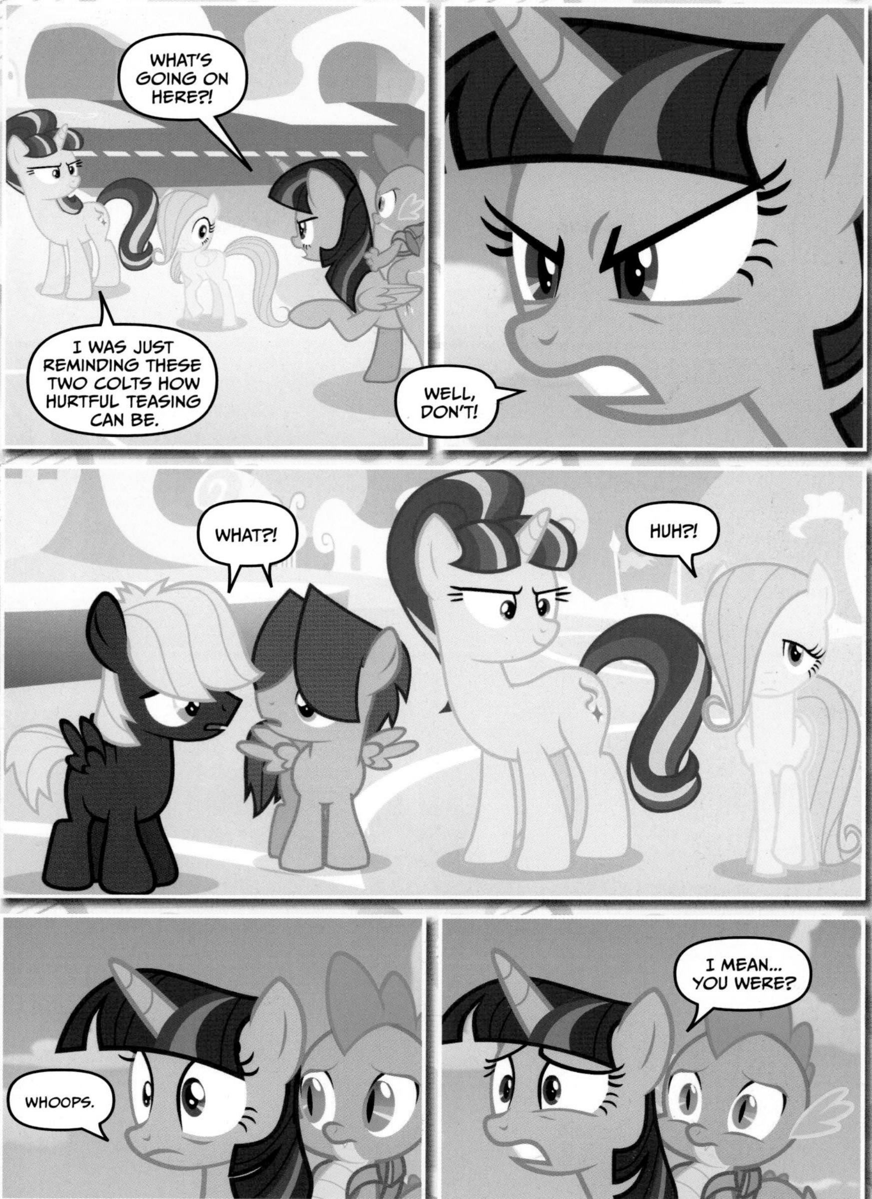
WHAT'S GOING ON HERE?!
I WAS JUST REMINDING THESE TWO COLTS HOW HURTFUL TEASING CAN BE.
WELL, DON'T!
WHAT?!
HUH?!
WHOOPS.
I MEAN... YOU WERE?

OF COURSE.

IN A WORLD WHERE EVERY PONY IS UNIQUE, SOME ARE BOUND TO FEEL MORE SPECIAL THAN OTHERS.

PUTT PUTT

BUT THAT ISN'T A LICENSE TO BE CRUEL IS IT?

NO. OF COURSE NOT.

ISN'T IT A SHAME WE DON'T LIVE IN A WORLD WHERE EVERYPONY IS EQUAL?

NO ONE WOULD EVER TEASE ANYONE THERE.

WOULDN'T THAT BE NICE?

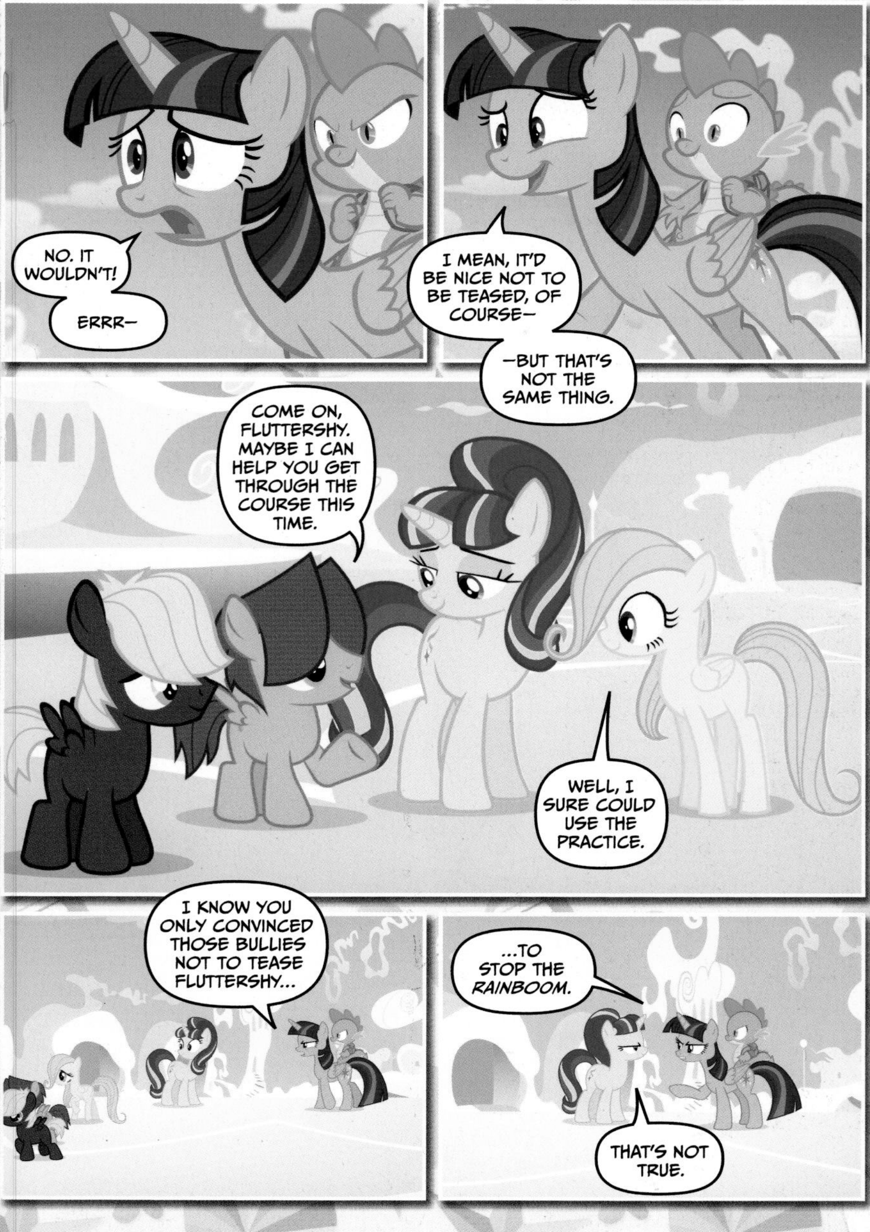
NO. IT WOULDN'T!
ERRR—
I MEAN, IT'D BE NICE NOT TO BE TEASED, OF COURSE—
—BUT THAT'S NOT THE SAME THING.
COME ON, FLUTTERSHY. MAYBE I CAN HELP YOU GET THROUGH THE COURSE THIS TIME.
WELL, I SURE COULD USE THE PRACTICE.
I KNOW YOU ONLY CONVINCED THOSE BULLIES NOT TO TEASE FLUTTERSHY...
...TO STOP THE *RAINBOOM.*
THAT'S NOT TRUE.

I CONVINCED THEM NOT TO BE BULLIES BECAUSE *EVERYPONY* SHOULD BE EQUAL.

STOPPING THE *RAINBOOM* IS JUST A *BONUS*.

FWOOOOOOOSH

LOOK!

FWOOOOOOOSH

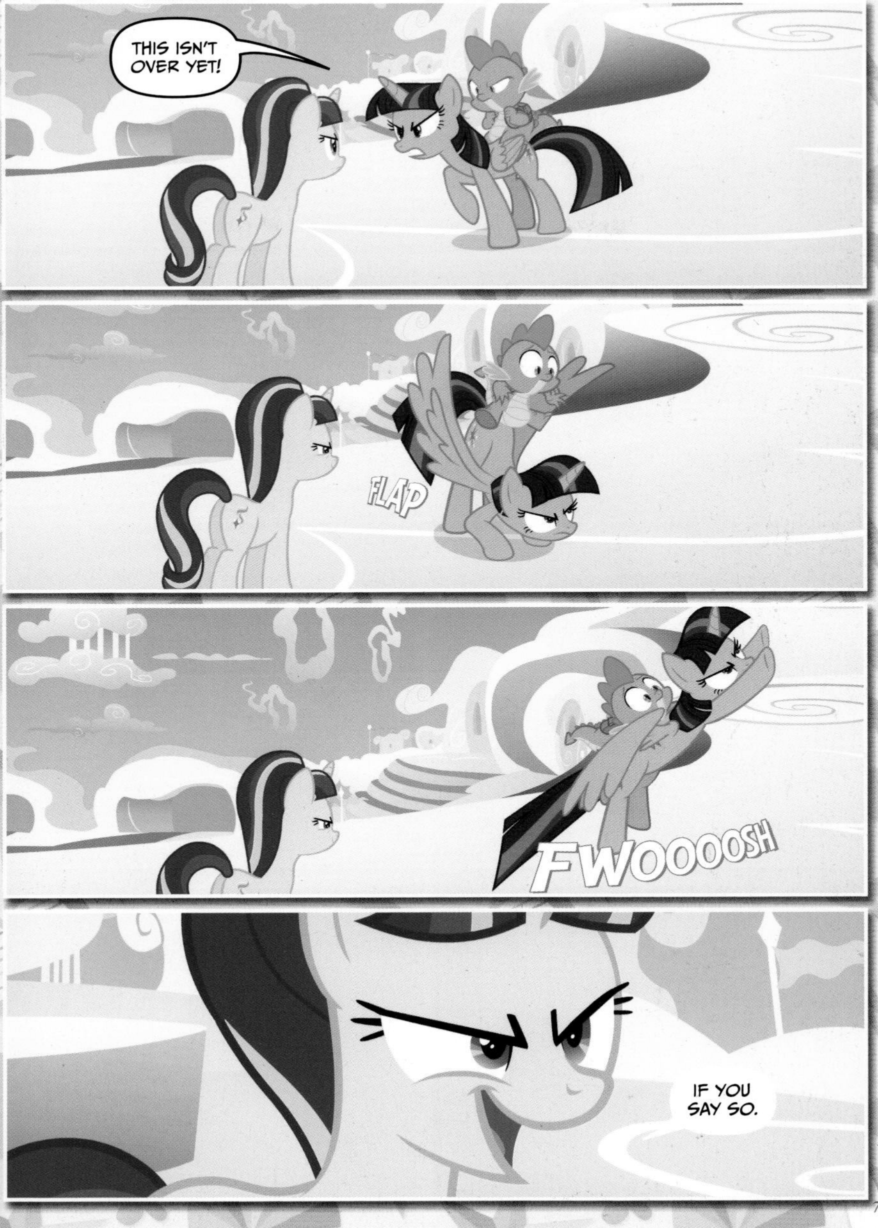
THIS ISN'T OVER YET!
FLAP
FWOOOOSH
IF YOU SAY SO.

HI!

FWOOOOOOSH

UMM... HI?

THINK YOU CAN STOP FOR A MINUTE?

SURE.

SKREEEEEEEE

BAMM

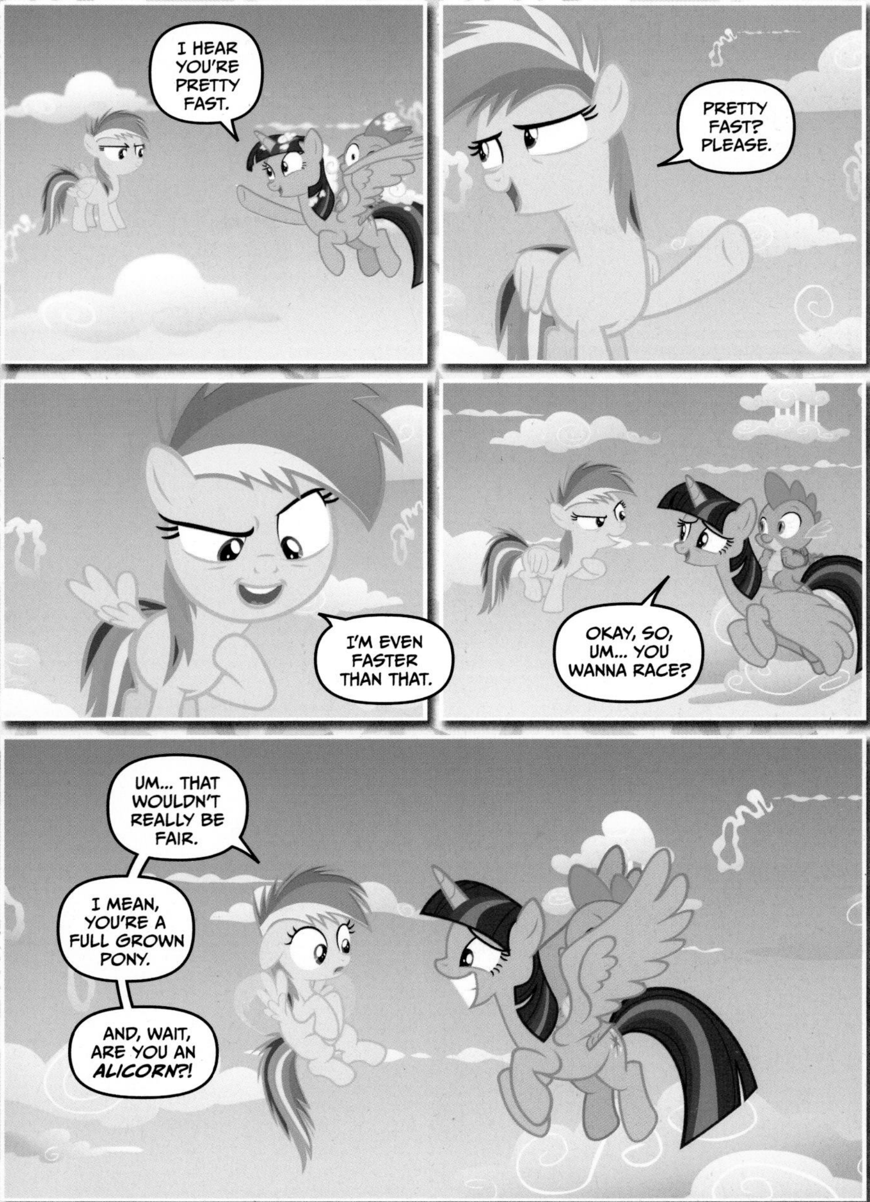
I HEAR YOU'RE PRETTY FAST.
PRETTY FAST? PLEASE.
I'M EVEN FASTER THAN THAT.
OKAY, SO, UM... YOU WANNA RACE?
UM... THAT WOULDN'T REALLY BE FAIR.
I MEAN, YOU'RE A FULL GROWN PONY.
AND, WAIT, ARE YOU AN *ALICORN*?!

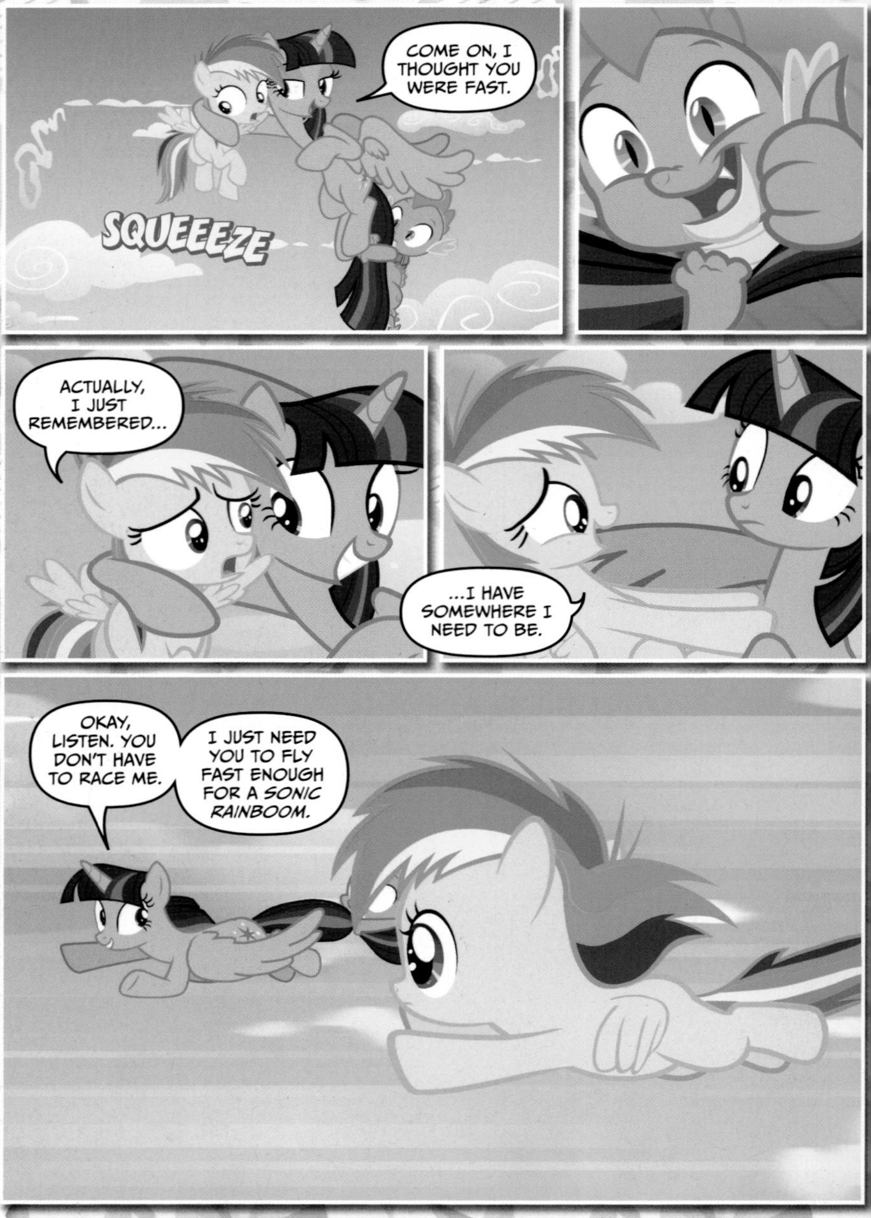
COME ON, I THOUGHT YOU WERE FAST.
SQUEEEEZE
ACTUALLY, I JUST REMEMBERED...
...I HAVE SOMEWHERE I NEED TO BE.
OKAY, LISTEN. YOU DON'T HAVE TO RACE ME.
I JUST NEED YOU TO FLY FAST ENOUGH FOR A *SONIC RAINBOOM.*

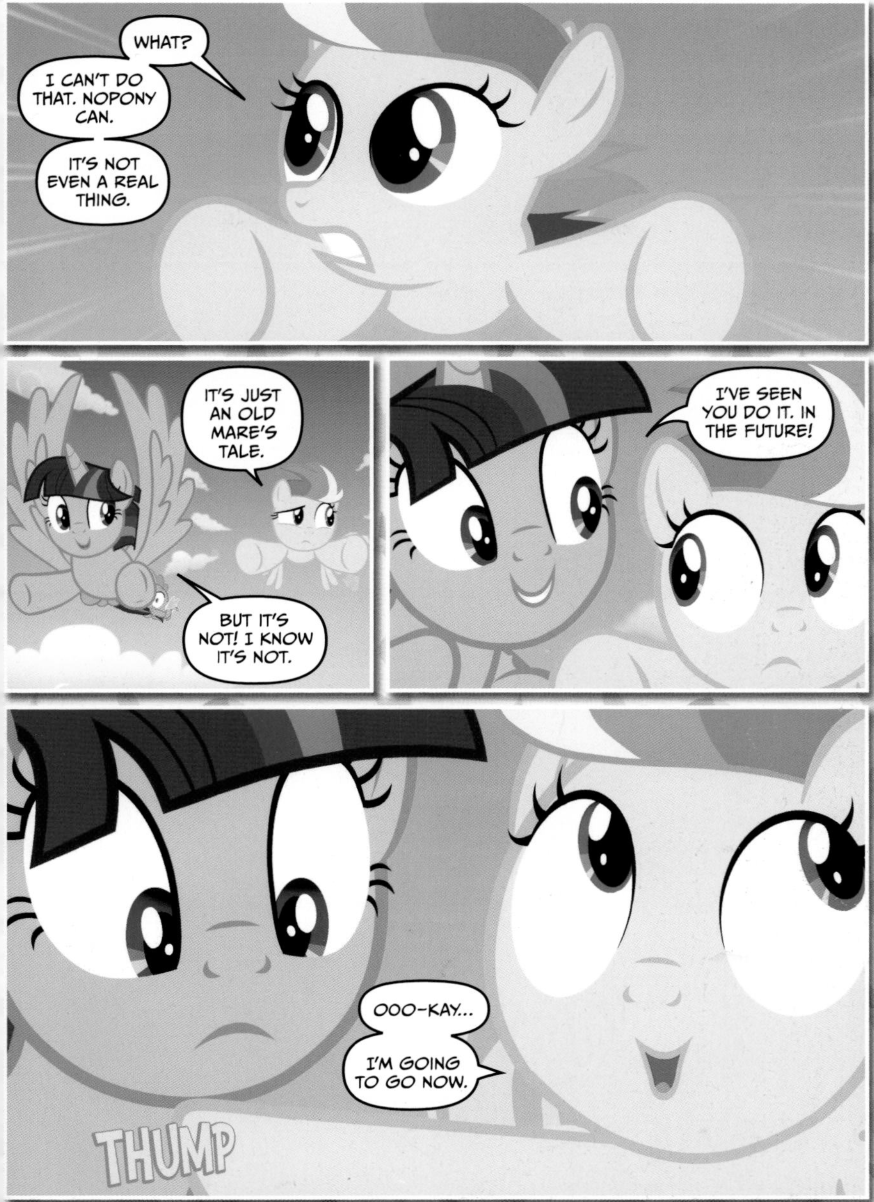
WHAT?
I CAN'T DO THAT. NOPONY CAN.
IT'S NOT EVEN A REAL THING.
IT'S JUST AN OLD MARE'S TALE.
BUT IT'S NOT! I KNOW IT'S NOT.
I'VE SEEN YOU DO IT. IN THE FUTURE!
OOO-KAY...
I'M GOING TO GO NOW.
THUMP

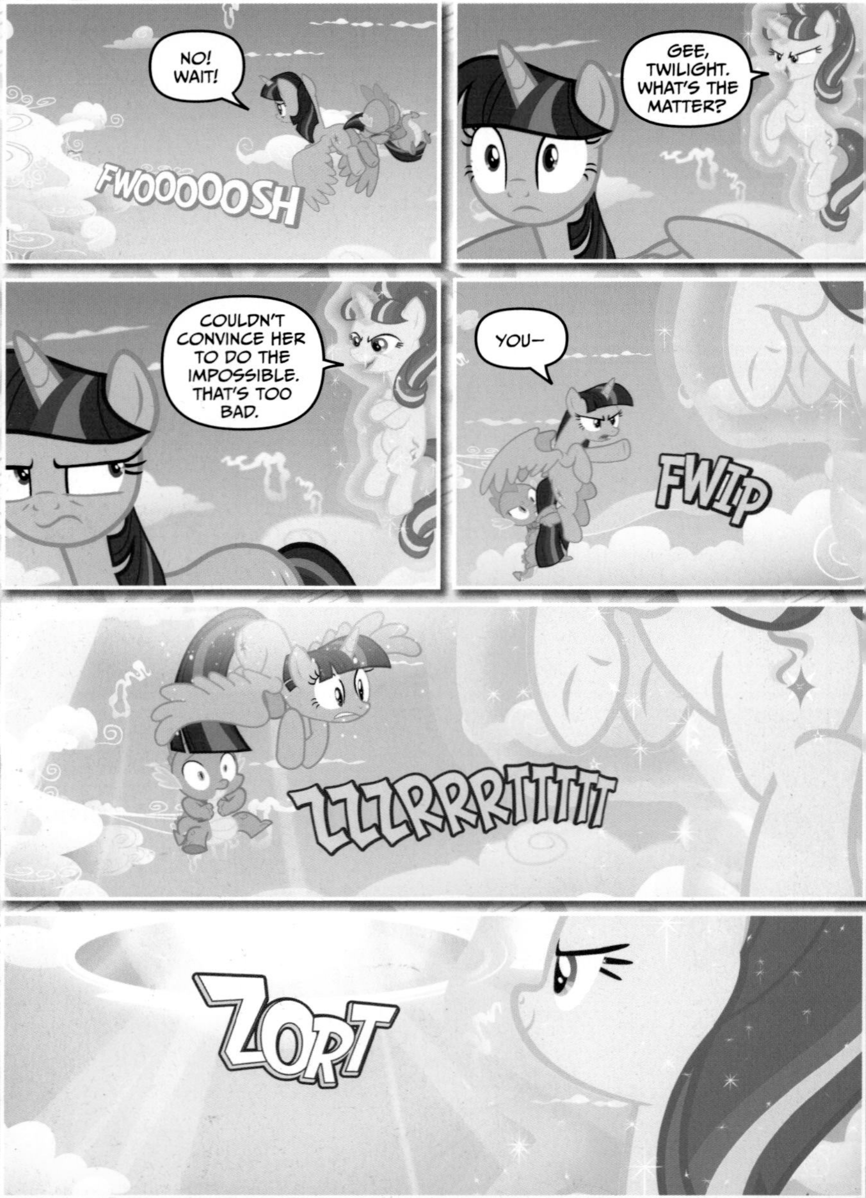

NO! WAIT!
FWOOOOOOSH
GEE, TWILIGHT. WHAT'S THE MATTER?
COULDN'T CONVINCE HER TO DO THE IMPOSSIBLE. THAT'S TOO BAD.
YOU—
FWIP
ZZZRRRTTTTT
ZORT

SMACK

UUURRRTTTT

VIPP

UNGH—

WELL, THAT DIDN'T WORK.

THIS IS GOING TO BE HARDER THAN I THOUGHT. WE'LL HAVE TO TRY AGAIN.

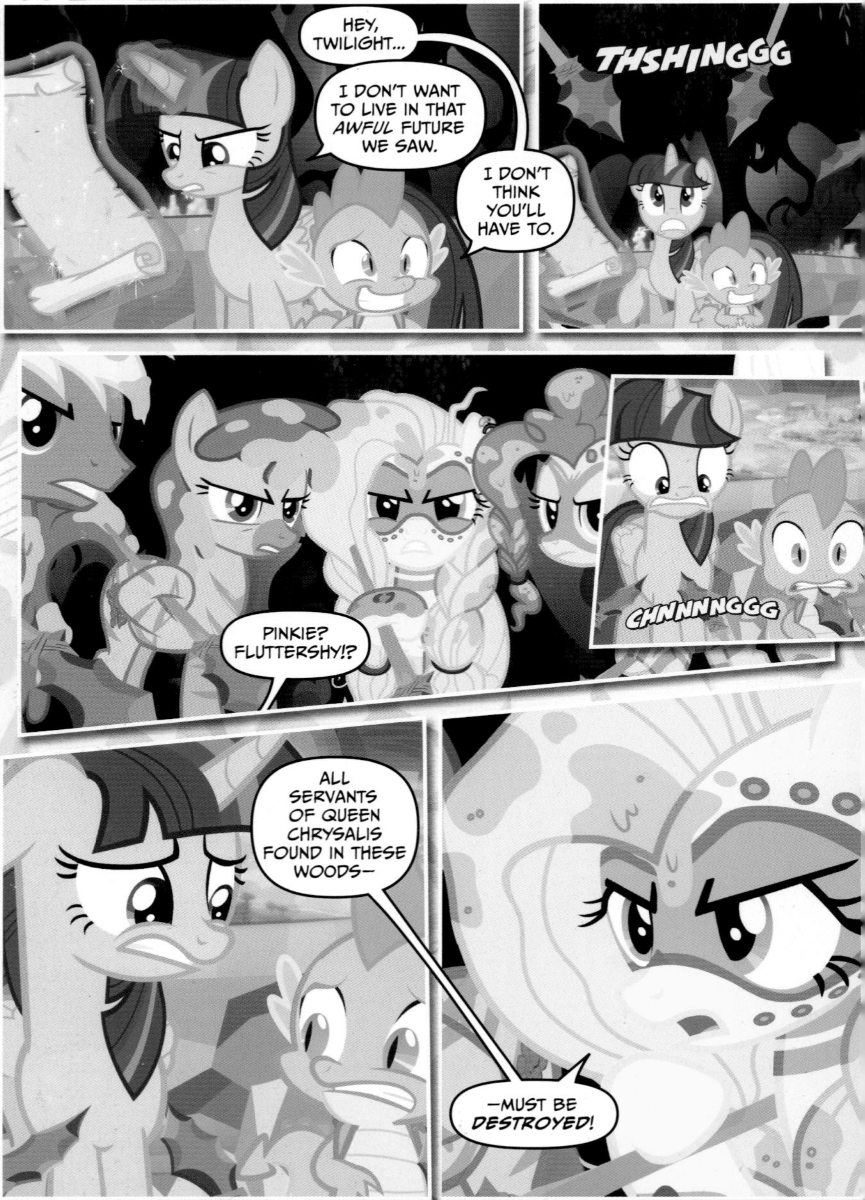
HEY, TWILIGHT...
I DON'T WANT TO LIVE IN THAT *AWFUL* FUTURE WE SAW.
I DON'T THINK YOU'LL HAVE TO.
THSHINGGG
CHNNNNGGG
PINKIE? FLUTTERSHY!?
ALL SERVANTS OF QUEEN CHRYSALIS FOUND IN THESE WOODS—
—MUST BE *DESTROYED!*

WAIT! WE'RE NOT CHANGELINGS! I'M A PONY! AND HE'S A DRAGON!

A LIKELY STORY!

DO SOMETHING DRAGONISH!

GULP!

BLE-WHOOOOSH

GASP!

THAT WORKS!

THE SERVANTS OF CHRYSALIS WILL DO ANYTHING—

—TO SAVE THEIR EVIL SKINS!

JAB JAB

STOP!

EVERYPONY TURNS TOWARDS THE SHOUTING.

IF THEY ARE CHANGELINGS, WE'LL SOON SEE...

...THOUGH I THINK THEY'RE NOT WHAT THEY APPEAR TO BE.

ZECORA! THANK YOU.

PLEASE, YOU HAVE TO LISTEN.

SHINK

SHINK

BENEATH THIS SALVE NO CHANGELING HIDES...

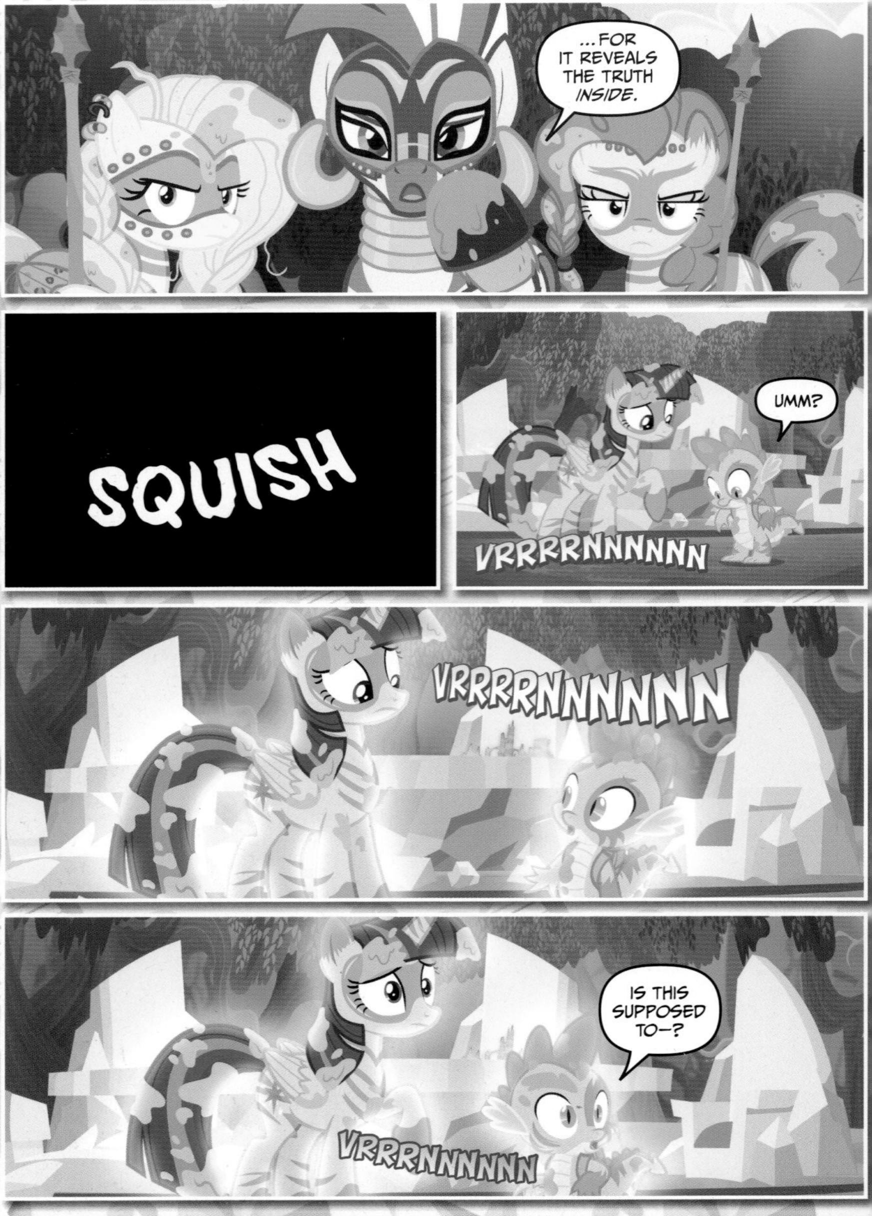

...FOR IT REVEALS THE TRUTH *INSIDE*.
SQUISH
UMM?
VRRRRNNNNNN
VRRRRNNNNNN
IS THIS SUPPOSED TO—?
VRRRNNNNNNN

GASP!

VIPP!

VOOOSH!

HMMM...

WHAT DOES IT MEAN?

THE MEANING IS FAR WORSE, I SEE.

FOR IT IS *WE* WHO SHOULD NOT BE.

I THINK I CAN EXPLAIN.

I'M SURE YOU CAN, BUT LET'S NOT TALK HERE.

CHRYSALIS AND HER ARMY WILL SOON DRAW NEAR.

A SHORT WHILE LATER...

THE CHANGELINGS TOOK OVER NOT LONG AGO, THOUGH I'LL WAGER IN YOUR WORLD THAT ISN'T SO.

CHRYSALIS AND HER ARMY TRIED TO TAKE OVER CANTERLOT, BUT MY FRIENDS AND I STOPPED HER.

THOSE FRIENDS AS YOU KNOW THEM ARE NOT HERE, ALAS.

BUT TELL ME HOW ALL *THIS* CAME TO PASS.

STARLIGHT GLIMMER. A PONY WHO TRAVELED BACK IN TIME TO STOP MY FRIENDS AND ME FROM EVER COMING TOGETHER.

AND IT IS THESE FRIENDS YOU HAVE IN LIFE, THAT KEEPS EQUESTRIA FREE FROM STRIFE?

BUT THIS IS THE SECOND TIME I'VE COME BACK AND THIS WORLD IS EVEN WORSE THAN THE LAST ONE.

IF STARLIGHT KEEPS DOING THE SAME THING IN THE PAST, HOW COULD THE PRESENT BE SO DIFFERENT?

I GUESS SO.

AH!

TIME IS A RIVER...

SPLOOSH

...WHERE EVEN THE TINIEST CHANGES...

...CAN LEAD TO A WATERFALL OF EFFECTS DOWNSTREAM.

THIS PART OF THE FOREST IS DARK AND DAMP—

ZECORA PUSHES SOME SHRUBS ASIDE...

—BUT IT'S DONE WELL TO HIDE OUR CAMP.

THIS WAY.

HI!

THIS IS COZY.

AIEEEEE—!!

SHAKE SHAKE

SNAP

PLEASE! YOU HAVE TO HELP US!

THE CHANGELINGS ATTACKED PONYVILLE.

WE BARELY ESCAPED WITH OUR LIVES!

RAINBOW DASH—

WHUMP

THE ONLY CHANGELING ATTACK I SEE, IS THE ONE THAT'S COME HERE LOOKING FOR ME.

IT'S TAKEN QUITE A WHILE TO FIND YOU—

—ZECORA!

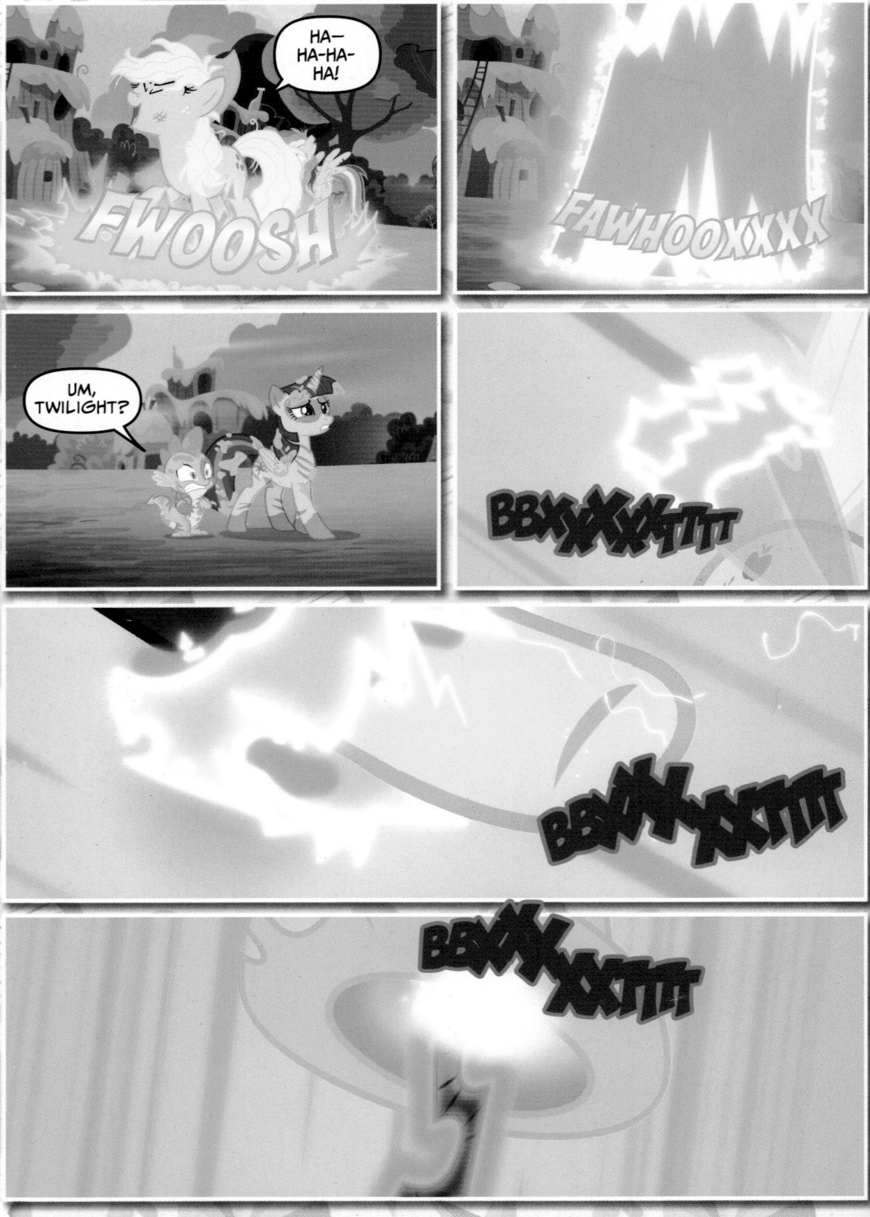
HA—
HA-HA-
HA!
FWOOSH
FAWHOOXXXX
UM,
TWILIGHT?

HA–HA–HA–HA!

WHAT A *LOVELY* VILLAGE YOU'VE CHOSEN TO STAGE YOUR LITTLE...

...RESISTANCE.

IT LOOKS ABSOLUTELY *DELICIOUS!*

AND YOU'RE VASTLY *OUTNUMBERED*

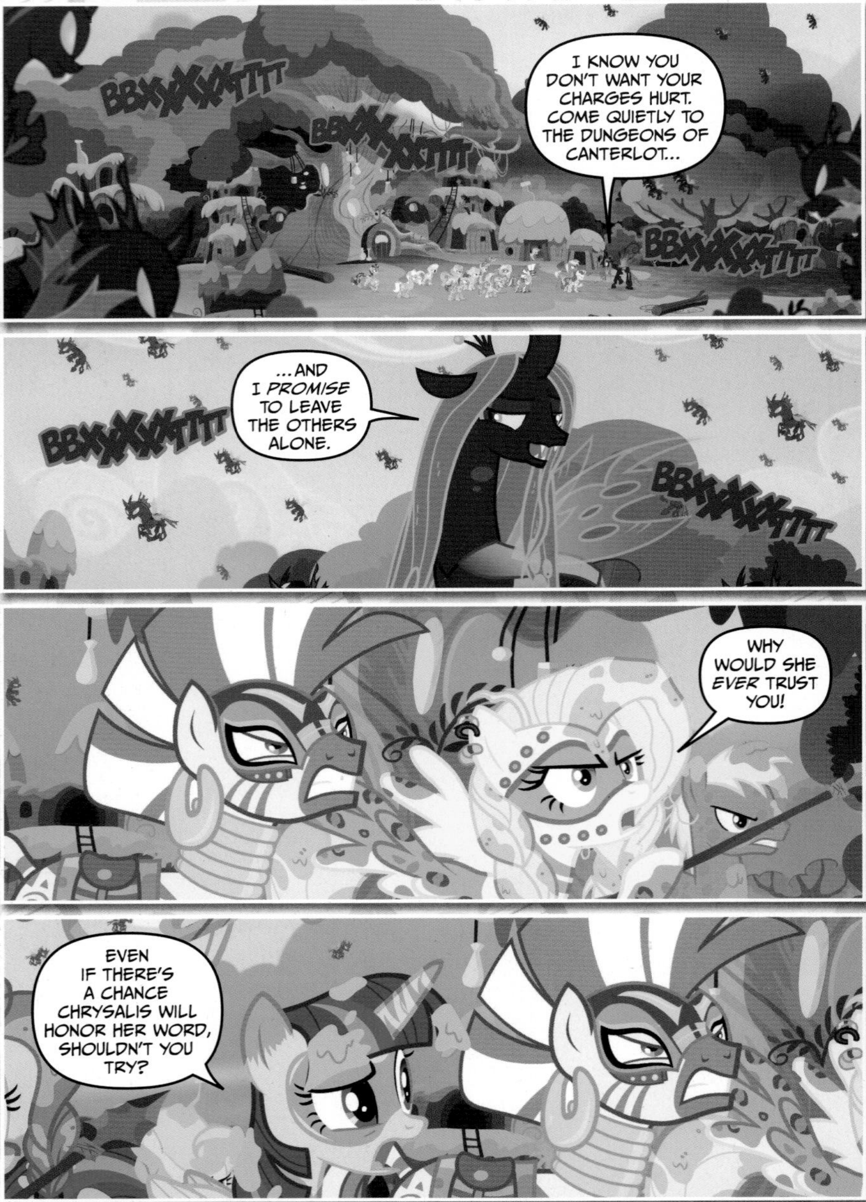
BBXXXXTTTT
BBXXXXXTTTT
I KNOW YOU DON'T WANT YOUR CHARGES HURT. COME QUIETLY TO THE DUNGEONS OF CANTERLOT...
BBXXXXXTTTT
...AND I *PROMISE* TO LEAVE THE OTHERS ALONE.
BBXXXXTTTT
BBXXXXXTTTT
WHY WOULD SHE *EVER* TRUST YOU!
EVEN IF THERE'S A CHANCE CHRYSALIS WILL HONOR HER WORD, SHOULDN'T YOU TRY?

RACE TO THE MAP WHILE WE HOLD OFF THEIR ATTACK.

STOP STARLIGHT AND PUT THE WHOLE WORLD BACK ON TRACK.

I WILL.

LET'S GO, SPIKE!

TIME TO MAKE A DECISION, ZECORA.

EVEN IF WHAT YOU ARE SAYING WERE TRUE—

—WE'D *NEVER* SURRENDER TO A CREATURE LIKE YOU.

CHARGE!

RUMBLE
RUMBLE

TIME TO FIGHT!

KRASH

BBXXXXTTT

XXORT

WHAMM

GRRRXXX-!

VORT

CLOP CLOP CLOP

BBXXXXTTT
BBXXXXTTT

CLOP CLOP CLOP

HURRY, TWILIGHT!

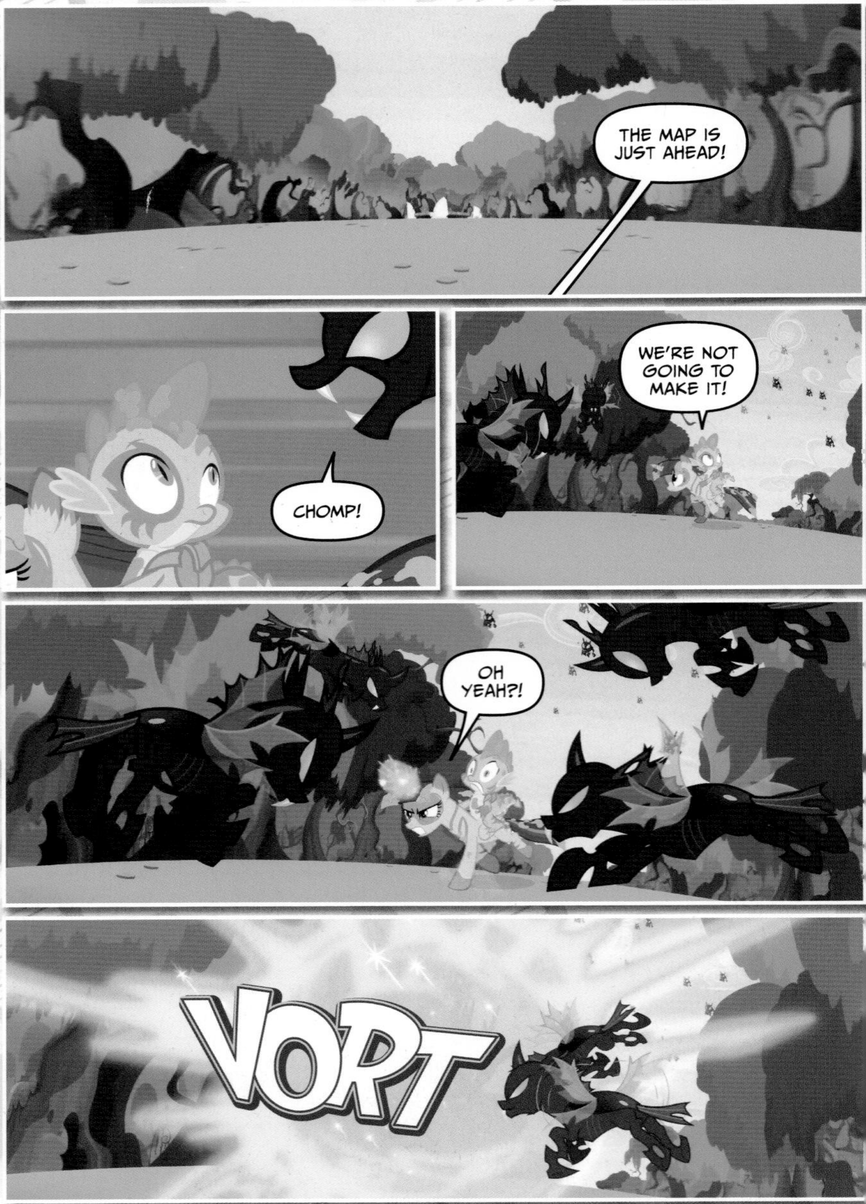
THE MAP IS JUST AHEAD!
CHOMP!
WE'RE NOT GOING TO MAKE IT!
OH YEAH?!
VORT

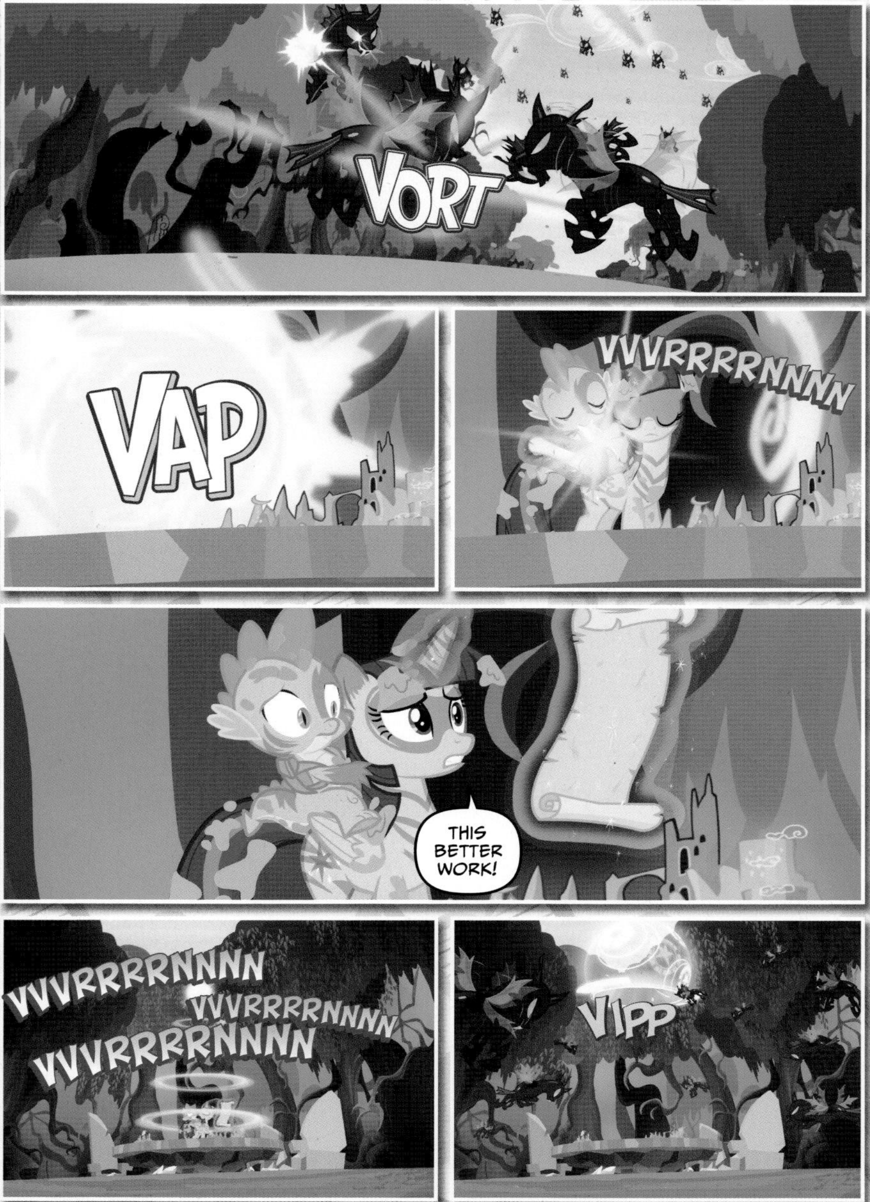
VORT
VAP
VVVRRRRNNNN
THIS BETTER WORK!
VVVRRRRNNNN
VVVRRRRNNNN
VVVRRRRNNNN
VIPP

VIPP

AHHHHH-!

THIS MIGHT HURT!

VVVVRRRRNNNN

HANG ON SPIKE!

VRRNNT

VORT

NOT THIS TIME, STARLIGHT...

VVVRRRRRNNNN

IS THERE ANYTHING I CAN—

—DO?

VRROOOOSH

VRROOOOOSH

VORT

VORT

STARLIGHT EFFORTLESSLY SIDESTEPS THE BLAST.

NOT BAD.

BUT IT'S GOING TO TAKE A LOT MORE THAN THAT!

LUCKY FOR YOU, THERE'S MORE WHERE THAT CAME FROM!

VORT VORT VORT

WHOA.

ZXXTT

ZXXTT

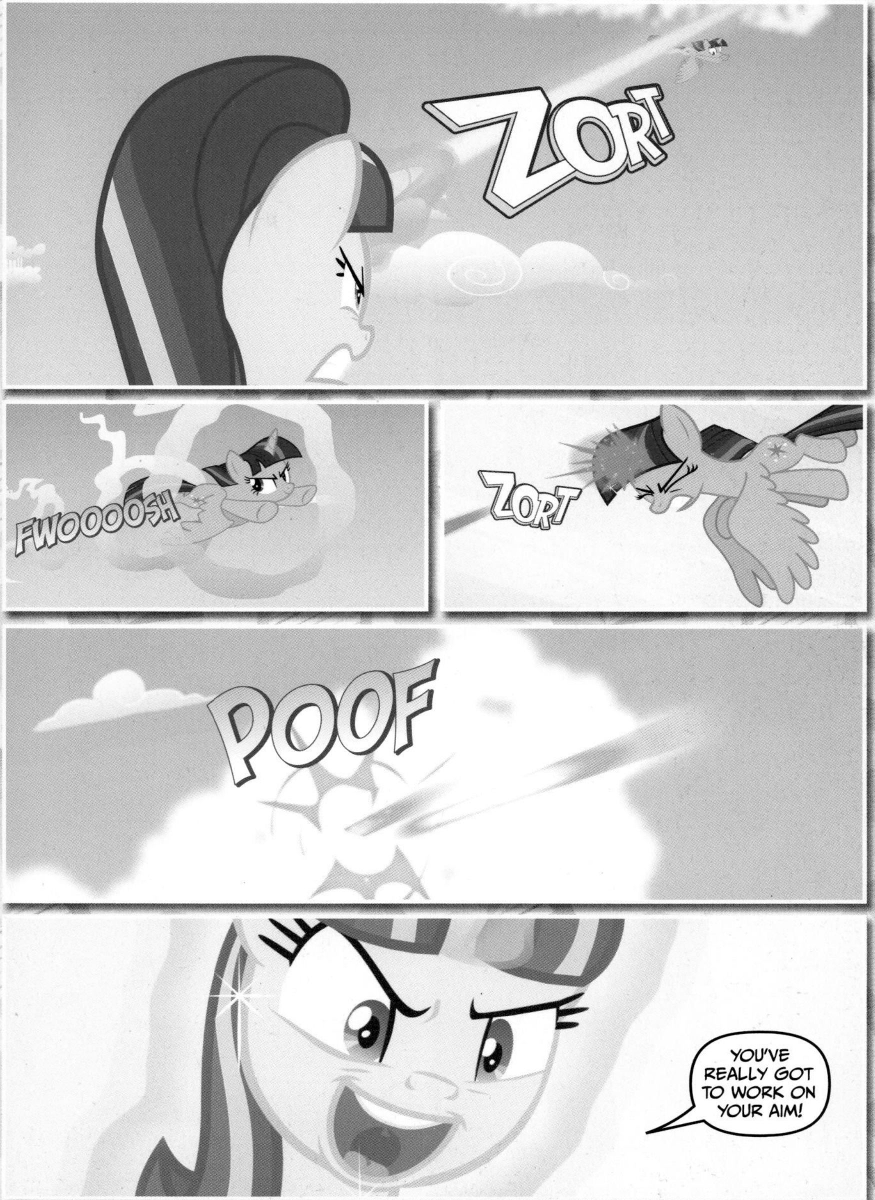
ZORT
FWOOOOOSH
ZORT
POOF
YOU'VE REALLY GOT TO WORK ON YOUR AIM!

XXORT

OH BOY.

YXXRRRTTTTZZZ

TWILIGHT AND STARLIGHT EXCHANGE MAGICAL BLOWS...

...WEARING EACHOTHER OUT IN THE PROCESS.

FWOOO-

HEY, WHAT'S THAT?!

VORT VIP

COOL!

OH NO!

WHAT ARE YOU ALL DOING? YOU HAVE TO FINISH YOUR RACE!

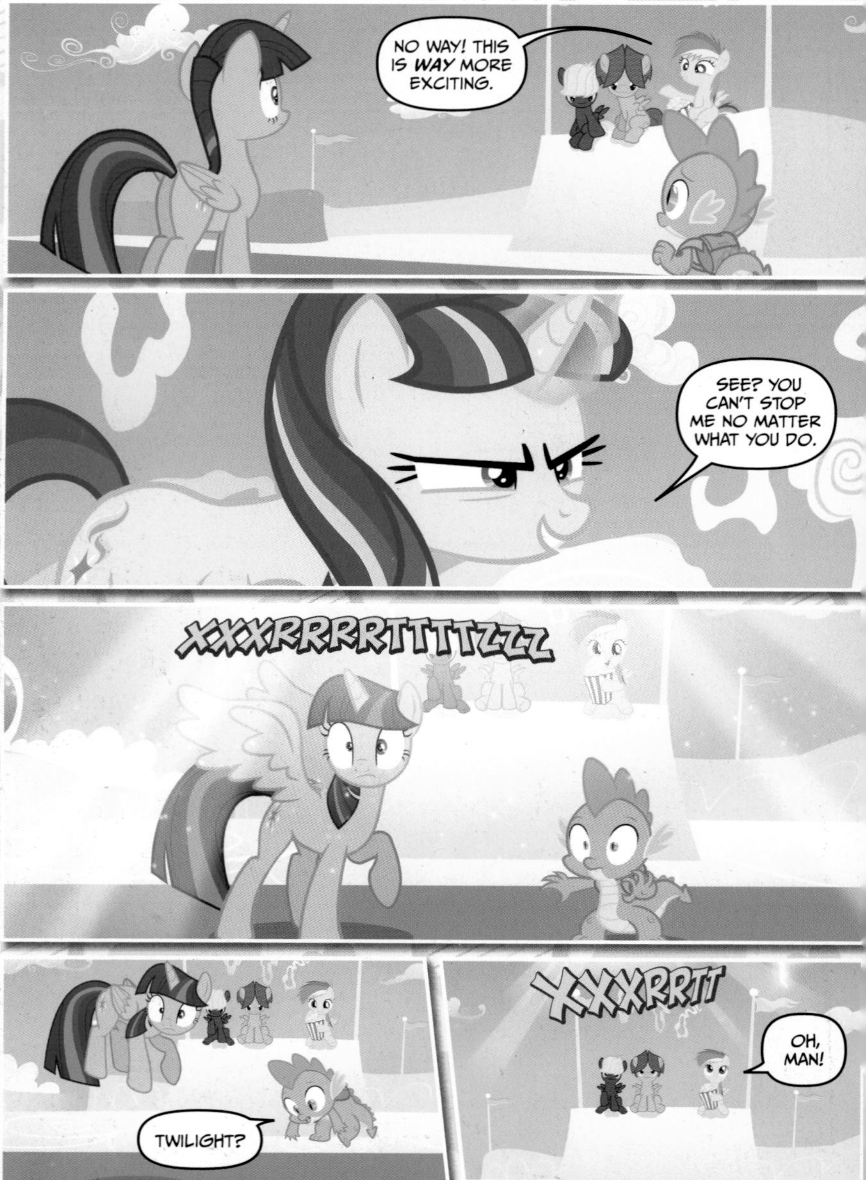

NO WAY! THIS IS *WAY* MORE EXCITING.
SEE? YOU CAN'T STOP ME NO MATTER WHAT YOU DO.
XXXRRRRRTTTTZZZZ
TWILIGHT?
XXXRRTT
OH, MAN!

WHUMP

UNGH. THAT'S STRANGE.

WELL, YOU OBVIOUSLY DON'T MEAN US FAILING, BECAUSE THAT'S BECOMING PRETTY ROUTINE.

NO. IT'S JUST THE OTHER TIMES WE'VE COME BACK IT'S BEEN DAY...

...BUT LOOK...

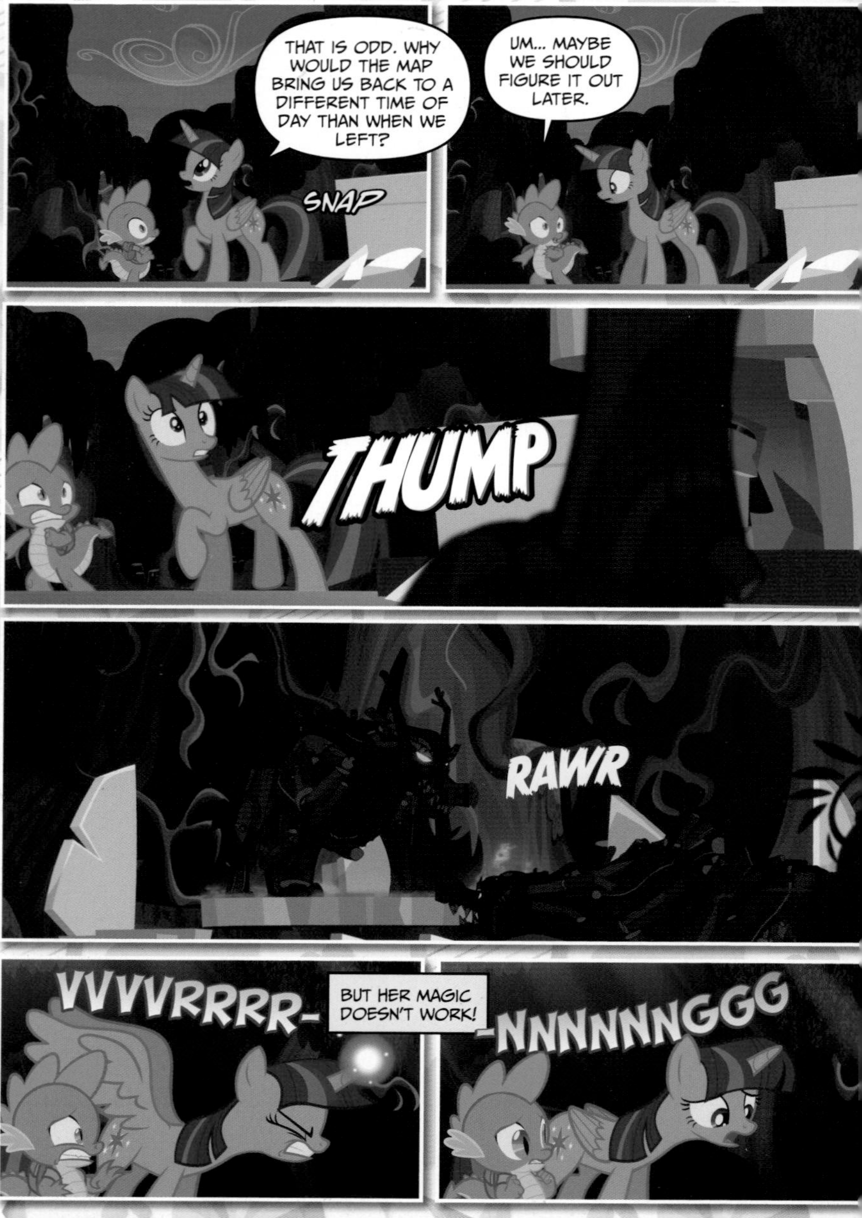
THAT IS ODD. WHY WOULD THE MAP BRING US BACK TO A DIFFERENT TIME OF DAY THAN WHEN WE LEFT?
SNAP
UM... MAYBE WE SHOULD FIGURE IT OUT LATER.
THUMP
RAWR
VVVVRRRR-
BUT HER MAGIC DOESN'T WORK!
-NNNNNNGGG

SNIFF

RUN!

HA-ROOOOO

WHERE ARE WE GOING?

ANYWHERE BUT HERE!

CLOP

CLOP CLOP

SKREEEE

THAT WAS TOO CLOSE!

WHOA.

THE CASTLE OF THE TWO SISTERS!

CLOP CLOP CLOP

BWHAM

SLAM

PHEW!

WOOSH
WOOSH
WOOSH
WOOSH

GULP!

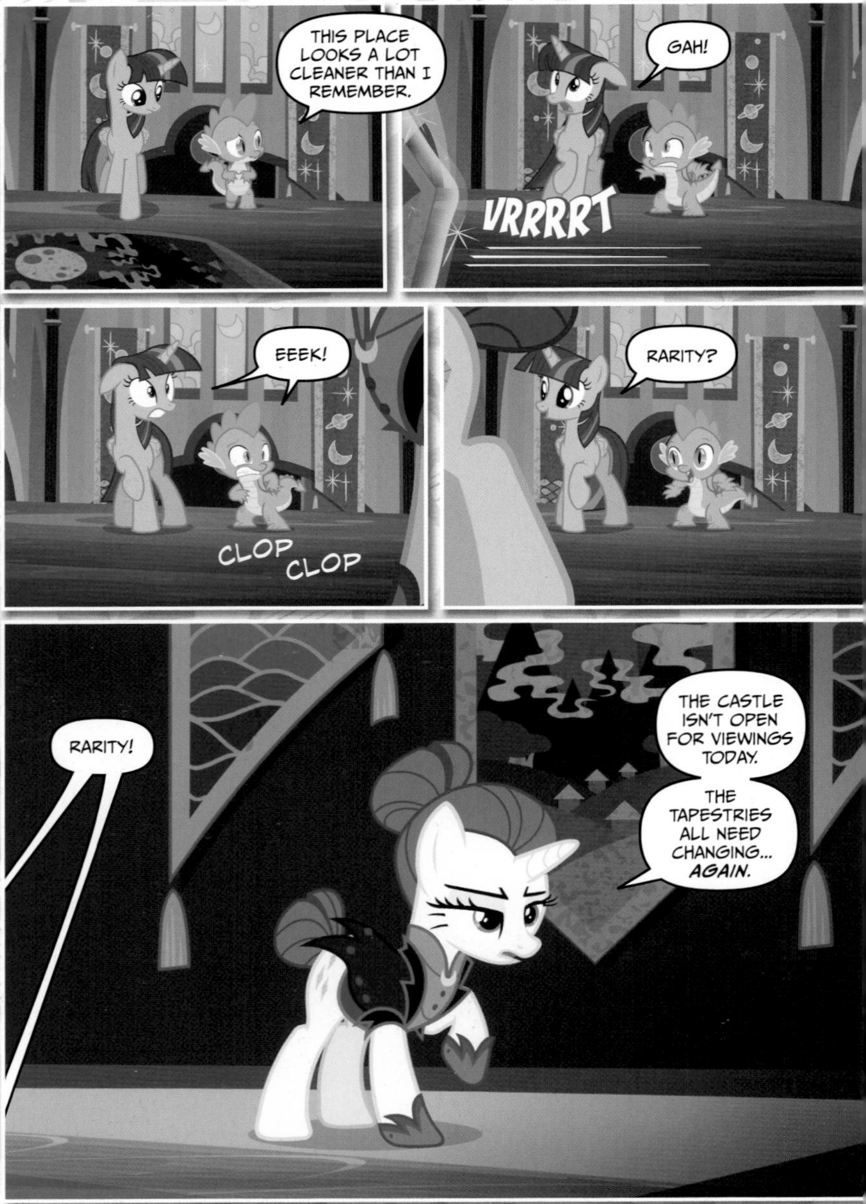

THIS PLACE LOOKS A LOT CLEANER THAN I REMEMBER.
GAH!
VRRRRT
EEEK!
CLOP CLOP
RARITY?
RARITY!
THE CASTLE ISN'T OPEN FOR VIEWINGS TODAY.
THE TAPESTRIES ALL NEED CHANGING... *AGAIN.*

RARITY, IT'S ME.

I DON'T SOCIALIZE WITH DRAGONS.

I DON'T KNOW *ANYPONY* WHO WOULD.

RARITY, YOU HAVE TO LISTEN TO ME.

THE FUTURE OF EQUESTRIA IS AT STAKE.

I DON'T KNOW HOW YOU KNOW MY NAME...

...BUT I'M FAR TOO BUSY TO ENTERTAIN SOME TOURIST'S RIDICULOUS FANTASIES.

I HAVE TO GET BACK TO THE MAP SO I CAN STOP STARLIGHT FROM CHANGING THE PAST BECAUSE EVERY *PRESENT* I COME TO IS WORSE THAN THE *LAST!*

TIME TRAVEL, YOU SAY?

WHERE DID THAT COME FROM?!

NOW *THAT'S* SOMETHING I'D LIKE TO SEE.

AH-HA-HA-HA-HA!

TELL ME HOW YOU CAME BY THIS MAGIC TO TRAVEL THROUGH TIME.

THE PRINCESS ASKED YOU A QUESTION!

AND UNLESS YOU WANT TO END UP IN THE DUNGEON, YOU'LL TELL HER WHAT SHE WANTS TO KNOW.

NO PONY IN *MY KINGDOM* BUT ME SHOULD POSSES A MAGIC POWERFUL ENOUGH TO CHANGE TIME.

RAINBOW DASH?

YOUR KINGDOM?

WHO ELSE?!

UM... CELESTIA, OF COURSE.

RAINBOW DASH AND ANOTHER GUARD SHARE A NERVOUS GLANCE.

...

HAH-HA-HAA!

MY SISTER—

—HAS BEEN IMPRISONED IN THE MOON FOR YEARS!

BUT IT'S NO LESS A FATE THAN SHE SENTENCED ME TO.

NOW. REVEAL TO ME THE SOURCE OF THIS TIME MAGIC.

ALL RIGHT, SPIKE.

WE HAVE NO CHOICE...

TWILIGHT, NO!

I CAN TAKE YOU TO IT, BUT YOU'LL HAVE TO GET PAST THE TIMBERWOLVES.

I AM THE *RULER* OF ALL OF EQUESTRIA. WOLVES.

DO YOU THINK I CAN'T DEAL WITH TIMBERWOLVES?

NO. I *KNOW* YOU CAN.

AND IF YOU'RE THINKING OF TRYING TO ESCAPE...

IT WOULD BE VERY UNFORTUNATE FOR YOUR FRIEND.

LATER THAT NIGHT...

HUMPF

BXXRRTT

SMASH

HOW DOES IT WORK?

A PONY FROM MY TIME USED A SPELL TO TRAVEL BACK AND CHANGE THE PAST.

AND NOW YOU WILL GIVE THIS SPELL TO ME.

WITH IT I WILL ENSURE THAT THE *ELEMENTS OF HARMONY* ARE NEVER FOUND AND MY REIN LASTS FOREVER!

BUT IT WON'T.

WHAT?!

IN MY WORLD, MY FRIENDS AND I FOUND THE ELEMENTS AND USED THEM TO DEFEAT YOU.

AND I WILL DO *EVERYTHING* IN MY POWER TO *BRING THAT WORLD BACK.*

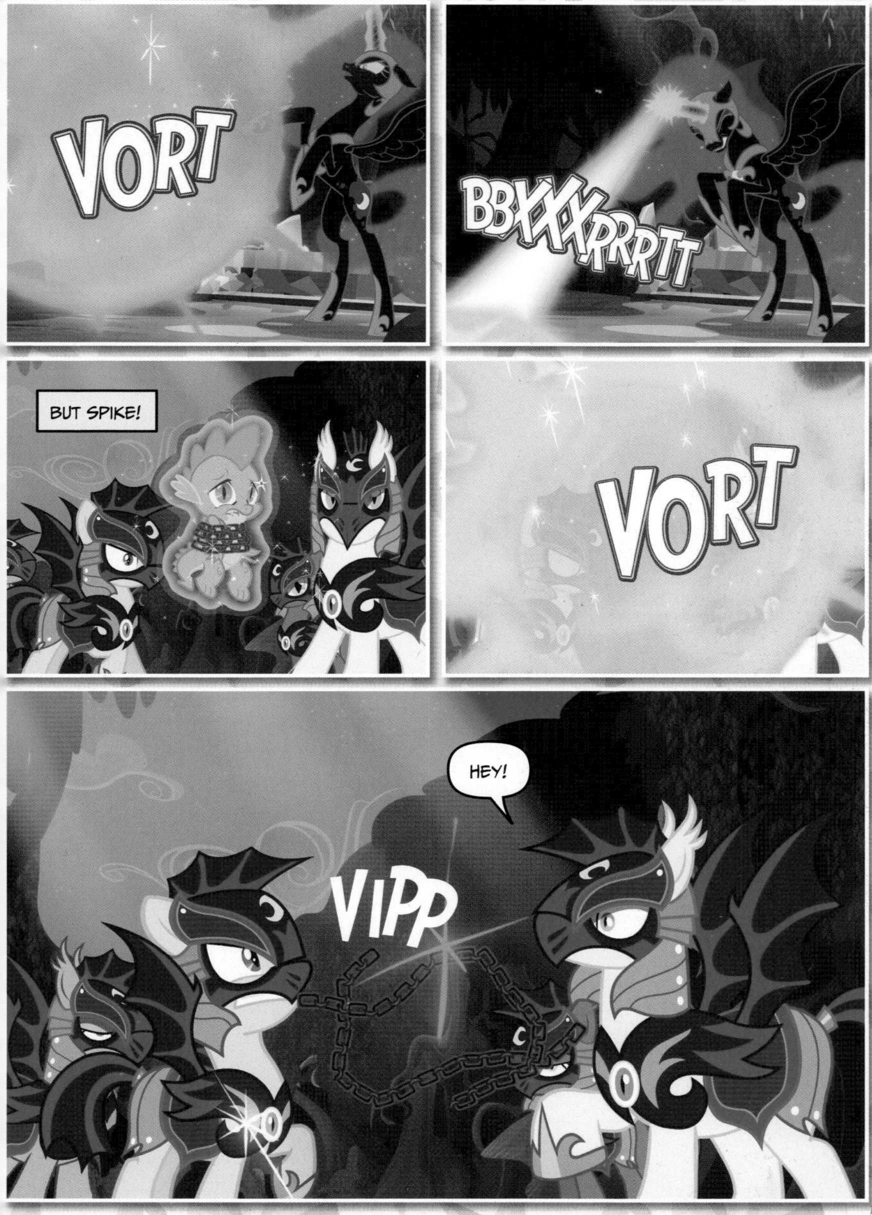
VORT
BBYXXRRRTT
BUT SPIKE!
VORT
HEY!
VIPP

VORT

TWILIGHT GETS BEHIND NIGHTMARE MOON, RIGHT ON TOP OF THE CUTIE MAP!

WHAT ARE YOU DOING?!

VRRRRNNNNNN

COME ON! FASTER!

VRRRRNNNNNN

NOOO!

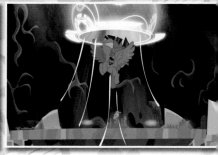

VRRRTTT

VAP

XXXRRTTTT

HNNNNG—!

VORT

TWILIGHT IS QUICK ON THE DRAW!

VRP

STALIGHT GLIMMER IS SHOCKED!

AND TRAPPED!

NOW MORE THAN EVER I KNOW HOW IMPORTANT IT IS TO STOP YOU.

XXXRRRTTT

XXXRRRTTTT

KRRRSSSHHHHHH

WELL, GOOD LUCK!

VVVRRRRXXXTTT

NOOOOO!

VAP

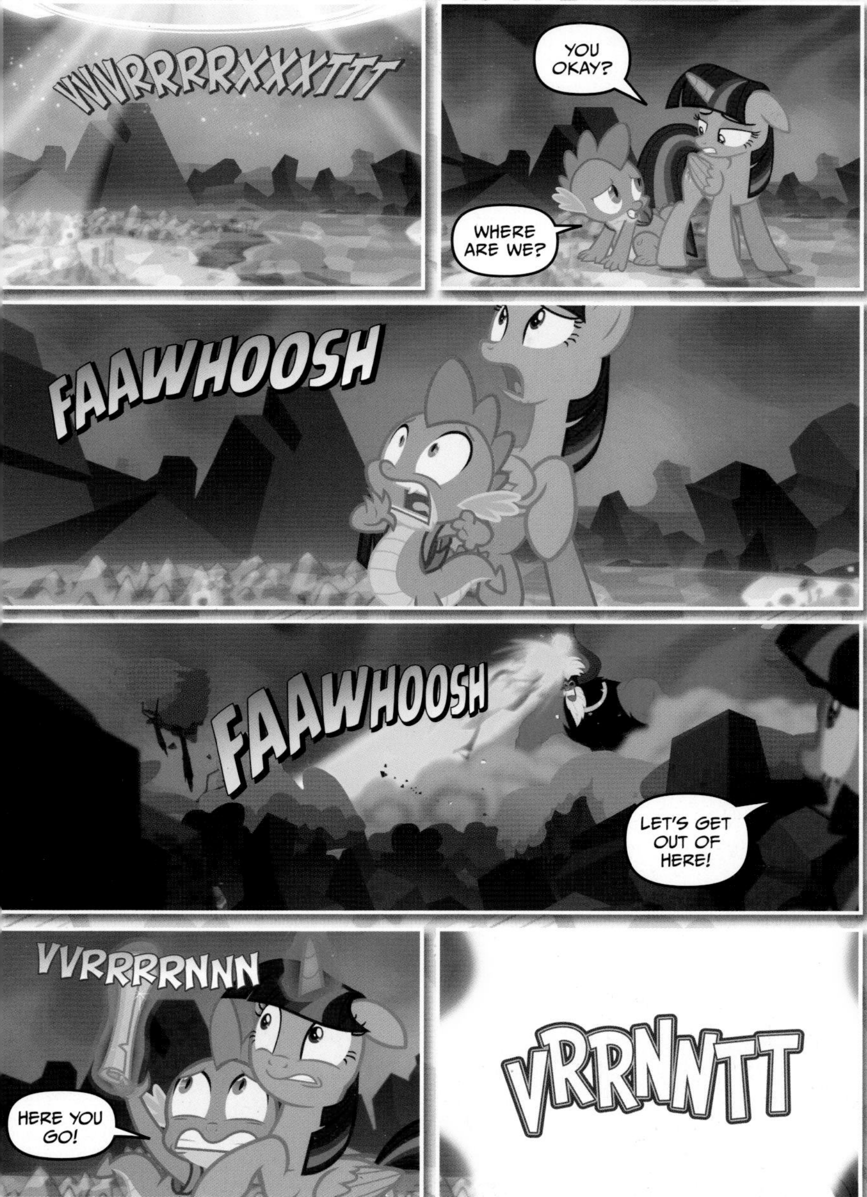
VVVRRRRXXXTTT
YOU OKAY?
WHERE ARE WE?
FAAWHOOSH
FAAWHOOSH
LET'S GET OUT OF HERE!
VVRRRRNNN
HERE YOU GO!
VRRNNTT

THERE SHE IS!

VORT

I THOUGHT WE'D SEE YOU AGAIN.

STARLIGHT STEPS OUT OF THE WAY...

VVVVRRRRRNNNNN

LOOKS LIKE YOU MISSED.

SEE YOU AROUND...

VVRRRRXXXXTTT

WHERE ARE WE NOW?!

HEHEHE, THIS IS SO MUCH FUN!

VVVRRRRXXXXTTT

LOOK OUT!

klank

OH NO!

RRRRPPP

RRRMMMBBBLLLL

THOSE TWO DID THIS?!

ZORT

VVWRRRXXXXTT

VIPPP

TWILIGHT EASILY MANEUVERS AROUND STARLIGHT'S BLAST.

SWOOSH

UP FOR ANOTHER RACE-ENDING FIGHT, TWILIGHT?

START

NO. YOU WERE RIGHT. I CAN'T STOP YOU.

START

XXXRRRTTT

START

VWRRRXXXTTT

BUT YOU CAN'T STOP ME FROM TRYING...

...AND WE COULD BE STUCK DOING THIS *FOR ALL OF ETERNITY.*

IF THAT'S WHAT IT TAKES TO KEEP YOU AND YOUR *FRIENDS* FROM GETTING YOUR *CUTIE MARK CONNECTION—*

—THEN I'M *GAME.*

BZRRRT

VRRXXXTTT

STARLIGHT, WHAT YOU'RE DOING GOES WAY BEYOND *CUTIE MARKS*.

EVERYTHING WE DO HERE IN THE PAST, EVEN THE SMALLEST CHANGE...

...CAN SNOWBALL INTO AN AVALANCHE OF TROUBLE FOR THE FUTURE.

SPLORT

NEXT I SUPPOSE YOU'LL TELL ME THAT THE FATE OF ALL OF EQUESTRIA HANGS IN THE BALANCE.

IT DOES!

SPARE ME YOUR OVER-BLOWN EGO.

NO GROUP OF FRIENDS, NOT EVEN *PRINCESS TWILIGHT'S*, IS THAT IMPORTANT.

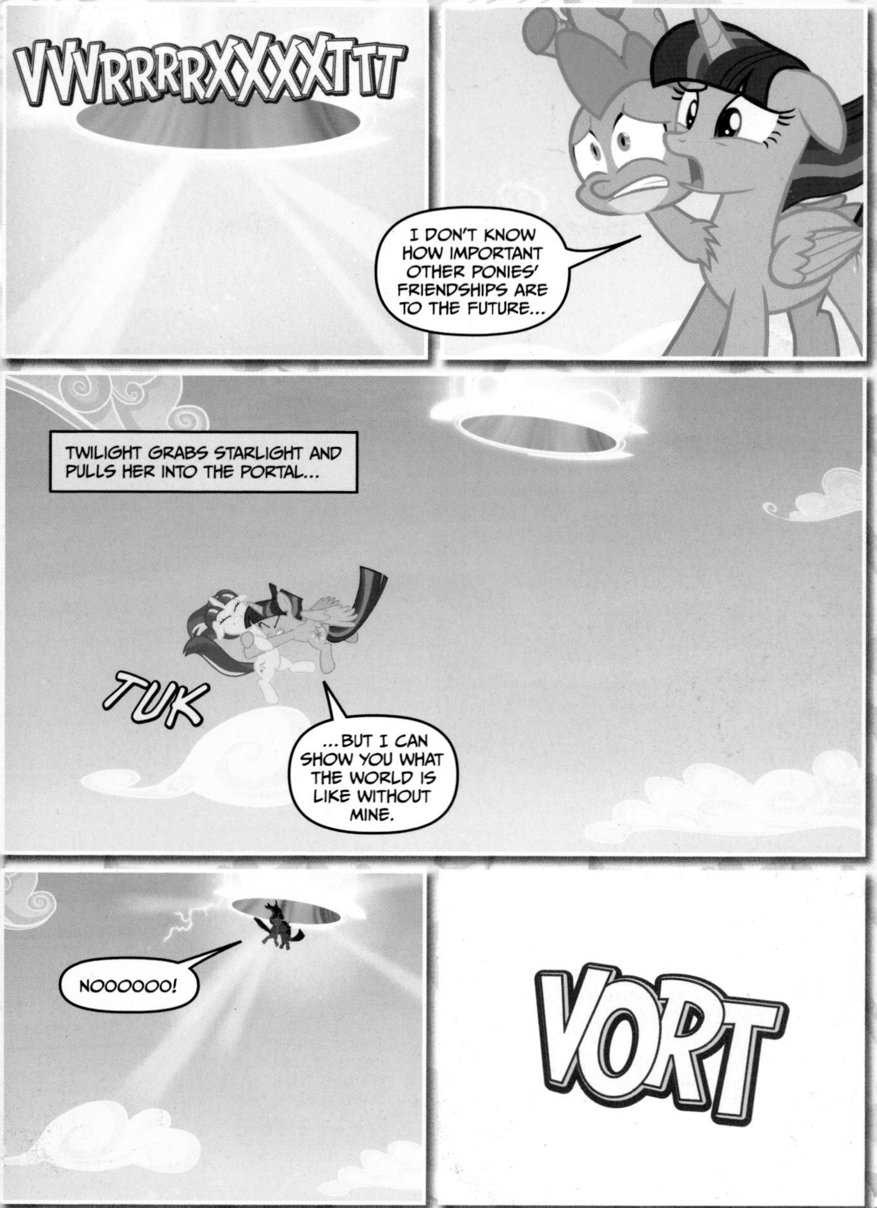
VVVRRRRXXXXTTT
I DON'T KNOW HOW IMPORTANT OTHER PONIES' FRIENDSHIPS ARE TO THE FUTURE...
TWILIGHT GRABS STARLIGHT AND PULLS HER INTO THE PORTAL...
TUK
...BUT I CAN SHOW YOU WHAT THE WORLD IS LIKE WITHOUT MINE.
NOOOOOO!
VORT

SOMEWHERE...

WOOOOOOSH

WOOOOOOSH

WHERE ARE WE?

THE FUTURE. OR RATHER, THE PRESENT.

BUT THERE'S NOTHING HERE!

I WISH I COULD SAY I WAS SURPRISED.

BUT EVERY WORLD I COME BACK TO IS WORSE THAN THE LAST.

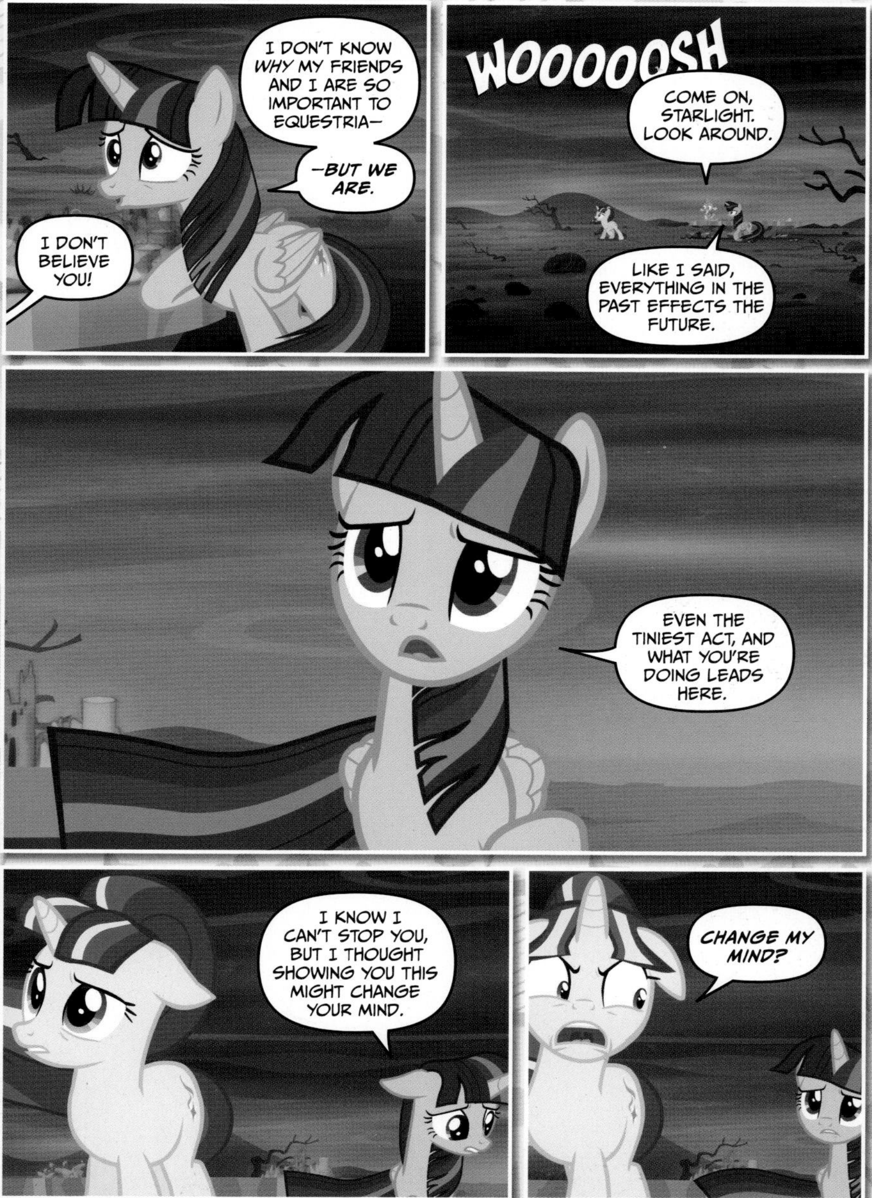
I DON'T KNOW WHY MY FRIENDS AND I ARE SO IMPORTANT TO EQUESTRIA—
—BUT WE ARE.
I DON'T BELIEVE YOU!
WOOOOOSH
COME ON, STARLIGHT. LOOK AROUND.
LIKE I SAID, EVERYTHING IN THE PAST EFFECTS THE FUTURE.
EVEN THE TINIEST ACT, AND WHAT YOU'RE DOING LEADS HERE.
I KNOW I CAN'T STOP YOU, BUT I THOUGHT SHOWING YOU THIS MIGHT CHANGE YOUR MIND.
CHANGE MY MIND?

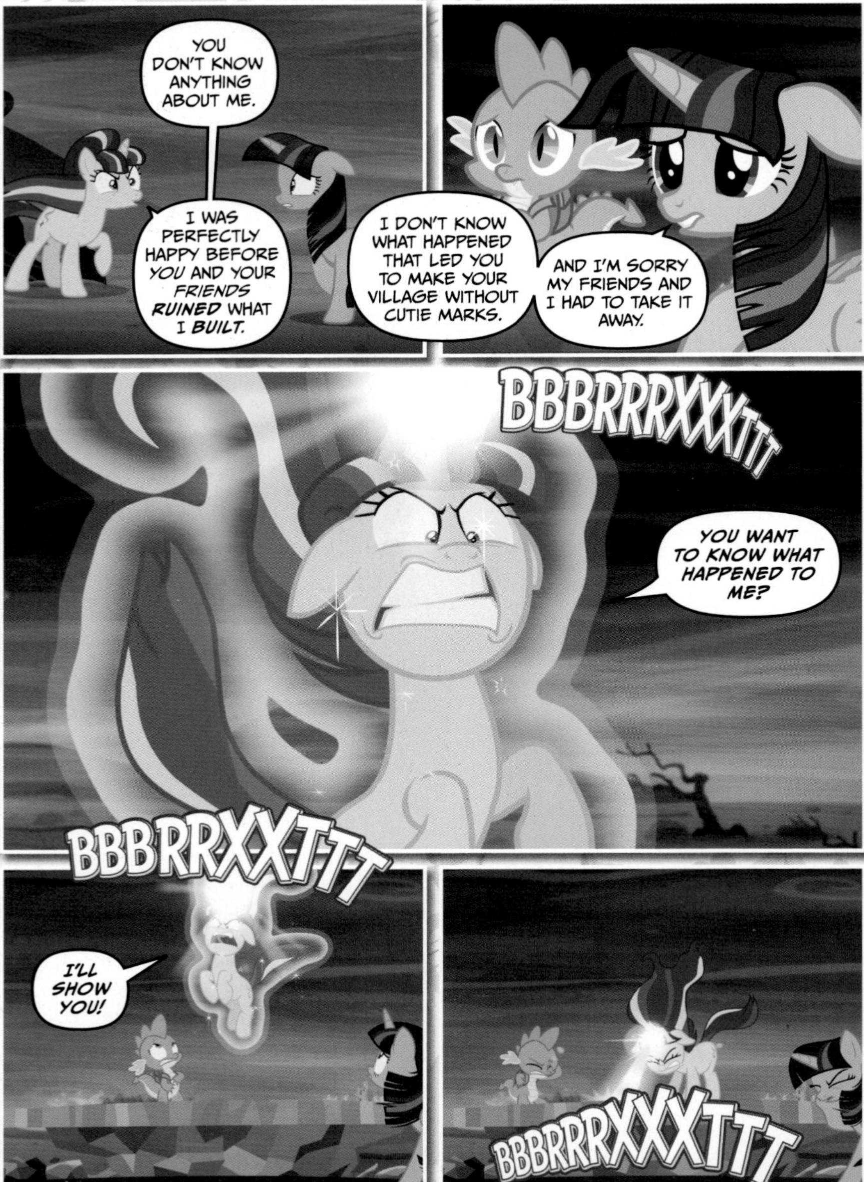
YOU DON'T KNOW ANYTHING ABOUT ME.
I WAS PERFECTLY HAPPY BEFORE *YOU* AND YOUR *FRIENDS* ***RUINED*** WHAT I ***BUILT***.
I DON'T KNOW WHAT HAPPENED THAT LED YOU TO MAKE YOUR VILLAGE WITHOUT CUTIE MARKS.
AND I'M SORRY MY FRIENDS AND I HAD TO TAKE IT AWAY.
BBBRRRRXXXTTT
YOU WANT TO KNOW WHAT HAPPENED TO ME?
BBBRRXXTTTT
I'LL SHOW YOU!
BBBRRRRXXXTTT

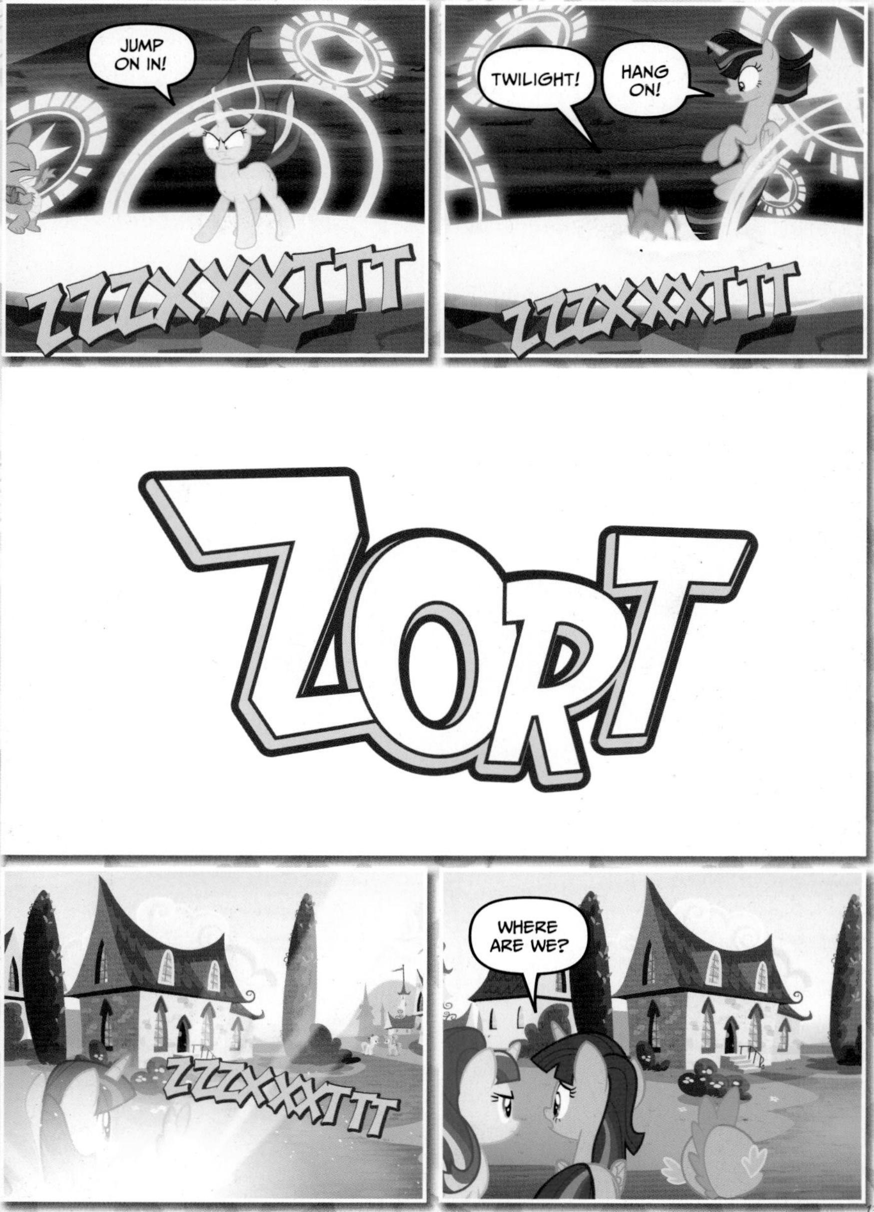
JUMP ON IN!
ZZZXXXTTT
TWILIGHT!
HANG ON!
ZZZXXXTTT
ZORT
ZZZXXXTTT
WHERE ARE WE?

THAT MAP OF YOURS IS CONNECTED TO EVERY PART OF EQUESTRIA...

...AND THIS PART IS MY HOME.

TEE-HEE!

"SUNBURST AND I DID EVERYTHING TOGETHER."

IN FACT, I DON'T REMEMBER US EVER BEING APART...

...UNTIL TODAY.

...UH OH!

LOOK OUT!

GAH—!

ZZZRRRRNNNN

ZZZRRRRNNNN

ZZZRRRRRRNNNNNNGGGGG

WHAT'S GOING ON?!

ZORT

MY CUTIE MARK!

OH YEAH!

I GOTTA SHOW EVERYPONY!

SUNBURST?

OH WOW!

CONGRATS!

GOOD JOB!

"AND JUST LIKE THAT, MY FRIEND WAS GONE."

HIS FAMILY RECOGNIZED HIS MAGICAL TALENT AND SENT HIM OFF TO CANTERLOT.

BUT YOU DON'T THINK—

BECAUSE OF HIS CUTIE MARK!

HE GOT HIS AND I DIDN'T.

HE MOVED ON AND I DIDN'T.

I STAYED HERE AND NEVER MADE ANOTHER FRIEND BECAUSE I WAS TOO AFRAID ANOTHER CUTIE MARK—

—WOULD TAKE THEM AWAY TOO!

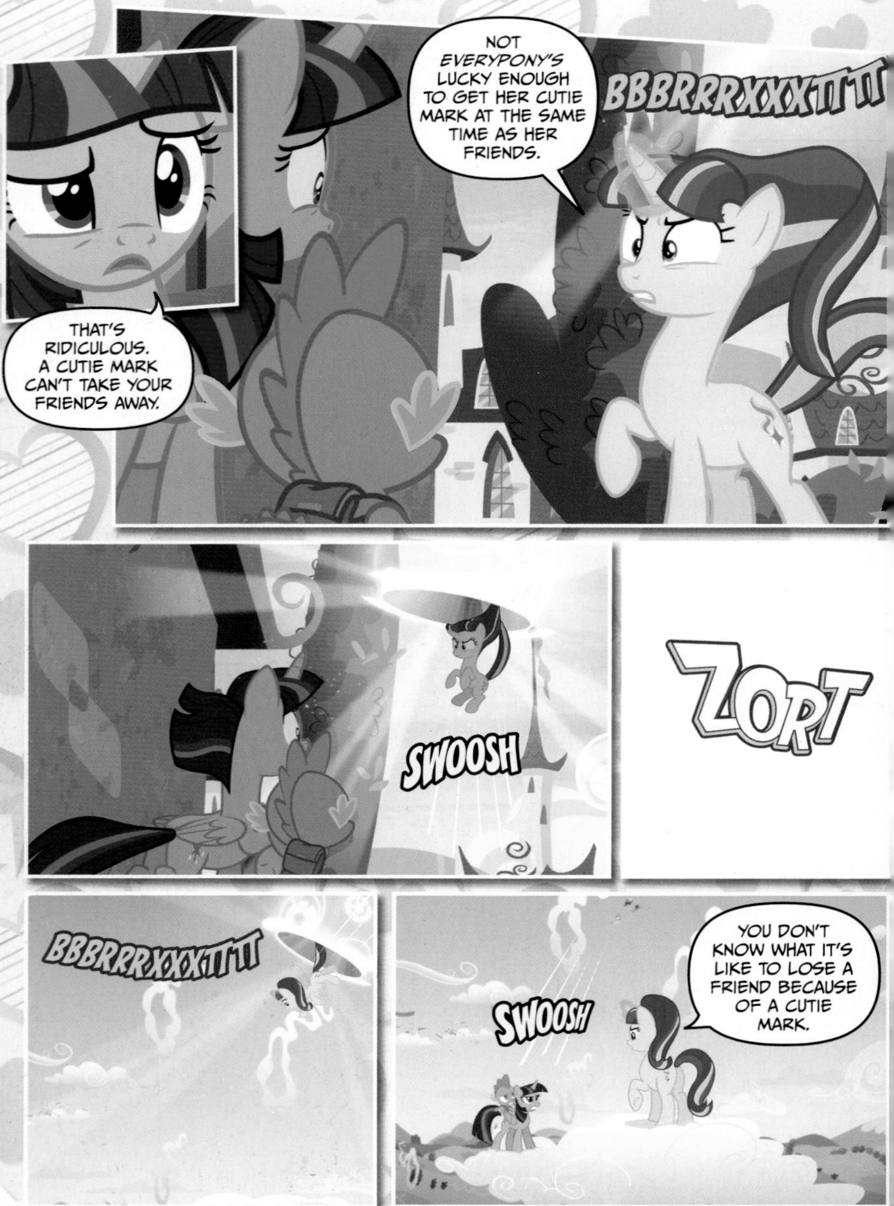
THAT'S RIDICULOUS. A CUTIE MARK CAN'T TAKE YOUR FRIENDS AWAY.
NOT EVERYPONY'S LUCKY ENOUGH TO GET HER CUTIE MARK AT THE SAME TIME AS HER FRIENDS.
BBBRRRXXXTTTT
SWOOSH
ZORT
BBBRRRXXXTTTT
SWOOSH
YOU DON'T KNOW WHAT IT'S LIKE TO LOSE A FRIEND BECAUSE OF A CUTIE MARK.

BUT ONCE I STOP THE *RAINBOOM* YOU WILL!

AND WHEN I DESTROY THIS SCROLL, THERE'LL BE *NO WAY FOR YOU* TO CHANGE IT!

VVVRRRXXXX

RRRR RIIIIP

STARLIGHT, YOU'RE RIGHT.

I DON'T KNOW WHAT YOU WENT THROUGH...

...BUT I DO KNOW YOU CAN'T DO *THIS*

I'VE SEEN WHERE THIS LEADS AND SO HAVE YOU.

I ONLY SAW WHAT YOU SHOWED ME.

WHO KNOWS WHAT WILL REALLY HAPPEN?

I DO. I'VE SEEN IT A DOZEN TIMES.

TRUST ME, THINGS DON'T TURN OUT WELL IN AN EQUESTRIA WITHOUT MY FRIENDS.

WHAT'S SO SPECIAL ABOUT YOUR *FRIENDS?*

HOW CAN A GROUP OF PONIES THAT ARE SO DIFFERENT BE SO IMPORTANT?

THE *DIFFERENCES* BETWEEN ME AND MY FRIENDS ARE THE VERY THINGS THAT MAKE OUR FRIENDSHIPS STRONG.

I THOUGHT SUNBURST AND I WERE THE SAME, BUT WE TURNED OUT DIFFERENT—

RRRR RIIIP

—AND IT TORE OUR FRIENDSHIP APART.

SO TRY AGAIN.

MAKE NEW FRIENDS.

AND IF SOMETHING THAT YOU CAN'T CONTROL HAPPENS THAT CHANGES THINGS...

...WORK THROUGH IT *TOGETHER.* THAT'S WHAT FRIENDSHIP IS.

AND IT'S NOT JUST MY FRIENDSHIPS THAT ARE IMPORTANT TO EQUESTRIA.

EVERYPONIES' ARE.

WHEN YOURS ENDED IT LED US HERE, BUT JUST IMAGINE ALL THE OTHERS THAT ARE OUT THERE...

WAITING FOR YOU IF YOU JUST GIVE THEM A CHANCE.

HOW DO I KNOW THEY WON'T ALL END THE SAME WAY?

I GUESS IT'S UP TO YOU TO MAKE SURE THEY DON'T.

BUT... BUT...

I CAN TRY.

STARLIGHT LETS GO OF THE SCROLL AND IT STARTS TO BLOW AWAY...

SNATCH

GOT IT!

AND RAINBOW DASH DOES THE *RAINBOOM!*

KABOOOOOM

FAAWWOOOOSHHH

WAY TO GO, RAINBOW DASH!

I KNEW SHE COULD DO IT.

IT WAS REAL?!

BBBRRRXXXTTT

LET'S GO HOME...

149

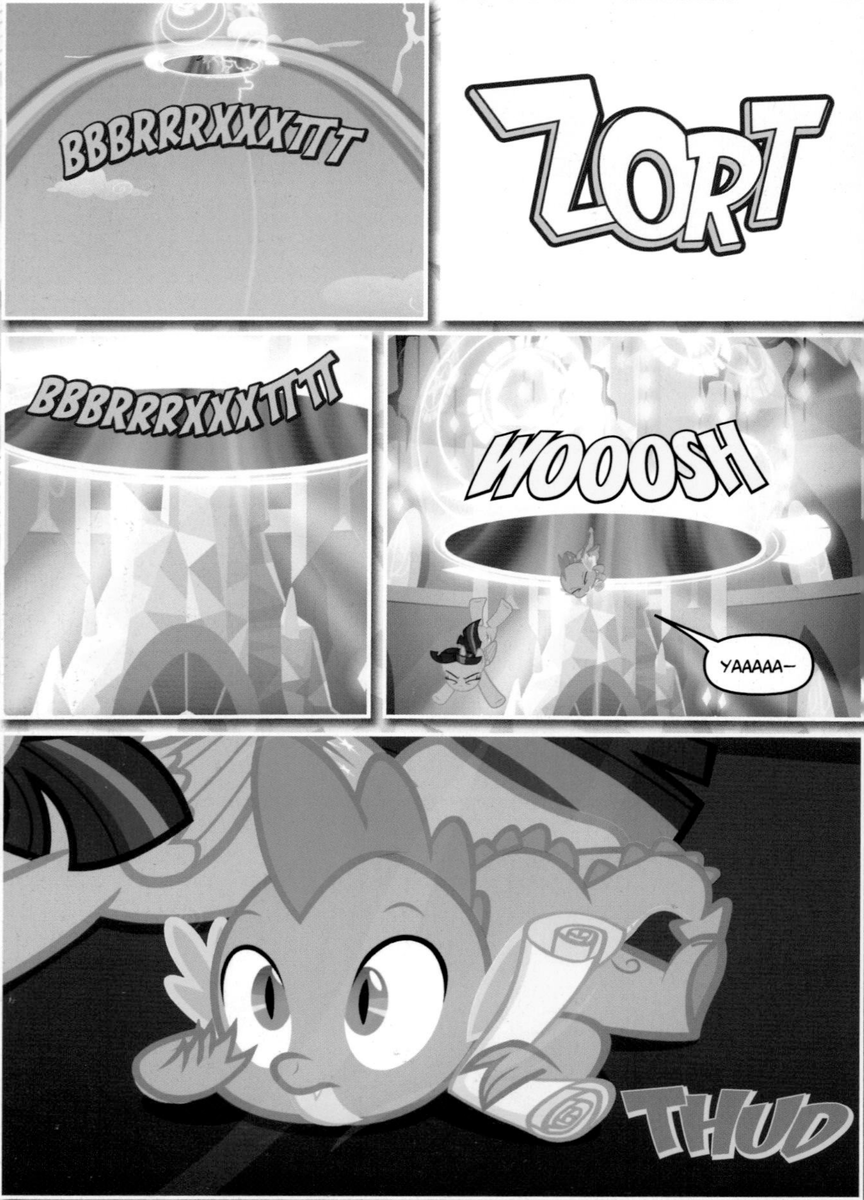
BBBRRRXXXTTT
ZORT
BBBRRRXXXTTT
WOOOSH
YAAAAA—
THUD

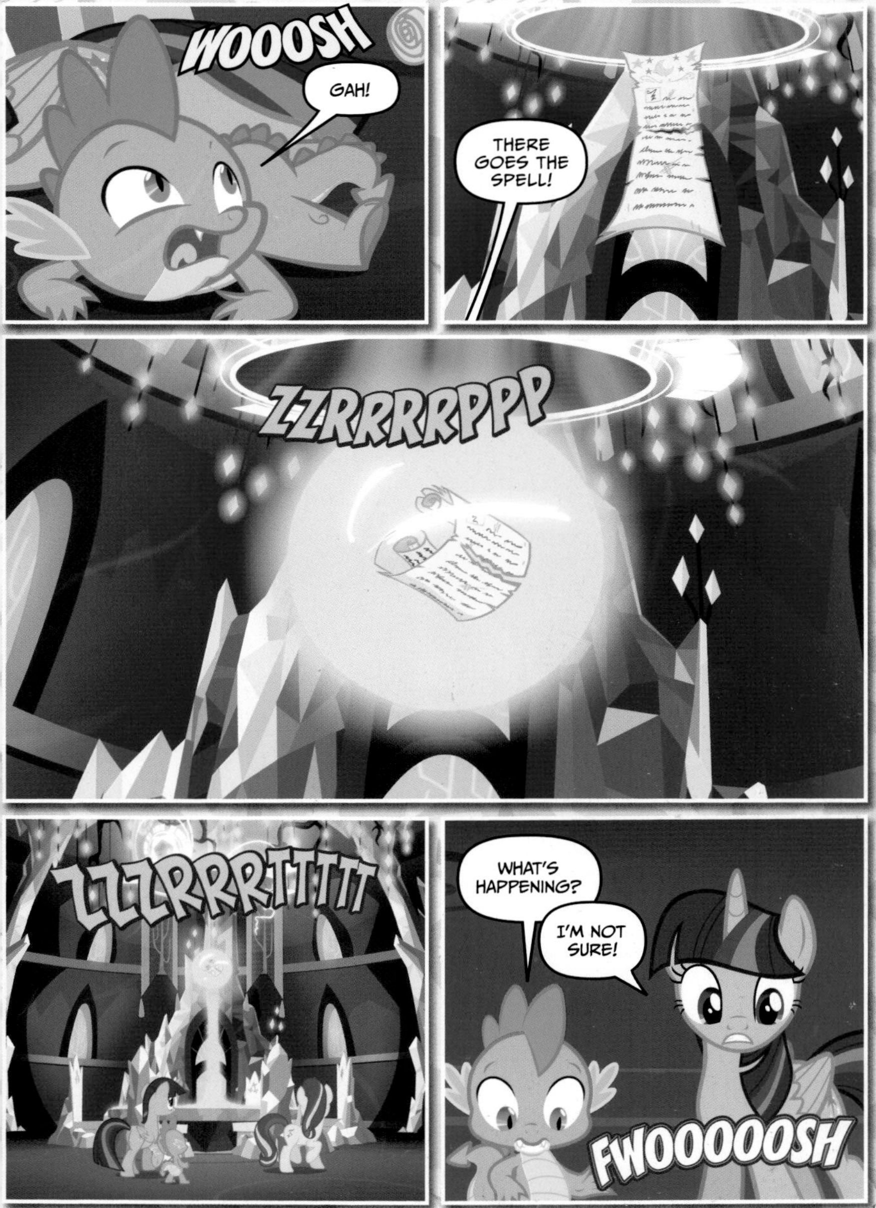
WOOOSH
GAH!
THERE GOES THE SPELL!
ZZRRRRPPP
ZZZRRRRTTTTT
WHAT'S HAPPENING?
I'M NOT SURE!
FWOOOOOSH

ZZZRRRTTTTT

WATCH OUT!

ZORT

VRRRRRRNNNNNN

ONE CASTLE OF FRIENDSHIP.

CHECK.

SMOOCH

WHUMP

WHAT IN EQUESTRIA WAS THAT?

IS EVERYPONY OKAY?

CAN YOU DO IT AGAIN!?

ONE GROUP OF AMAZING FRIENDS.

CHECK.

YEP, SPIKE. IT LOOKS LIKE WE'RE HOME.

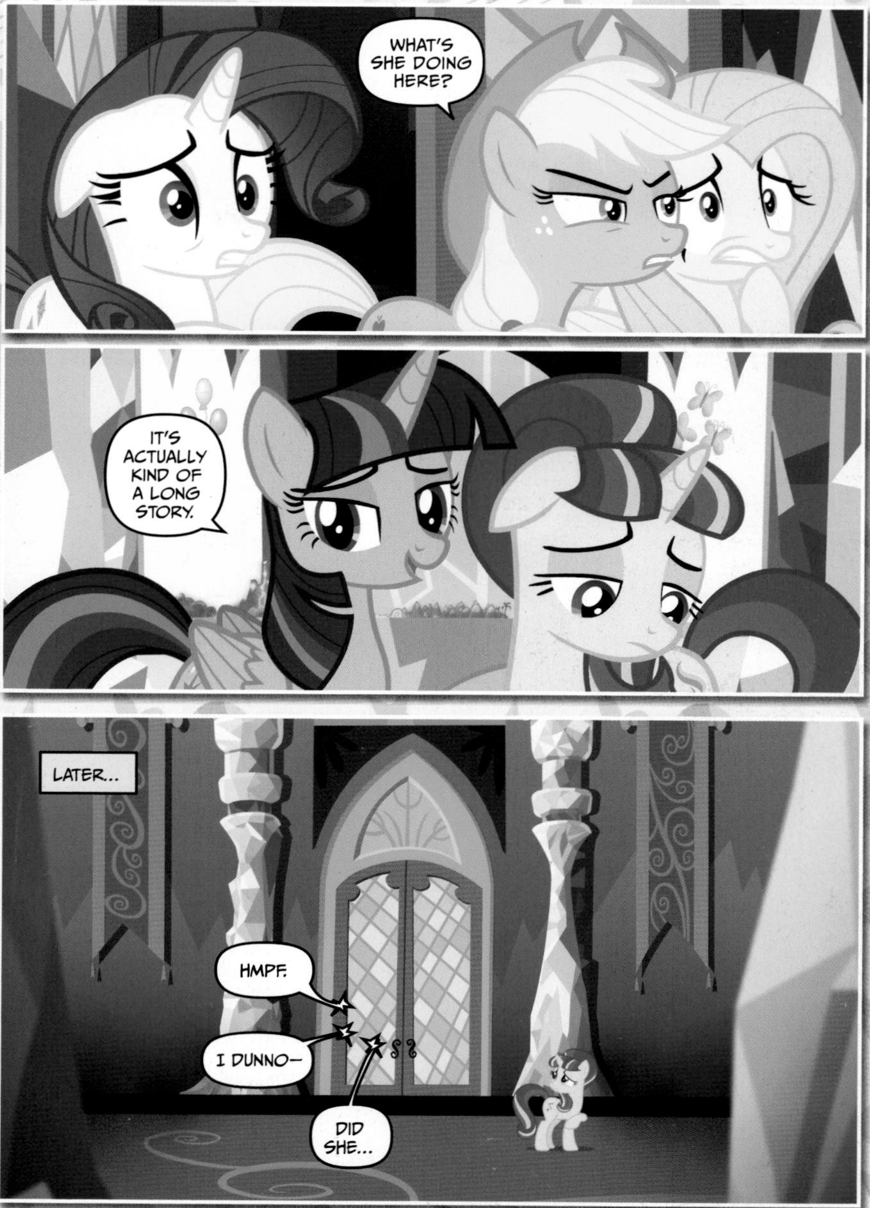
WHAT'S SHE DOING HERE?
IT'S ACTUALLY KIND OF A LONG STORY.
LATER...
HMPF.
I DUNNO—
DID SHE...

I MEAN, I KNEW MY RAINBOOM WAS AWESOME...

...BUT I NEVER THOUGHT ALL OF EQUESTRIA DEPENDED ON IT.

OR ON US!

I THINK IT'S MORE THAN THAT.

I THINK FRIENDSHIP CONNECTS ALL OF EQUESTRIA...

...AND UNDOING ONE GROUP OF FRIENDS MADE ALL OF ITS MAGIC LESS POWERFUL.

I CAN'T BELIEVE Y'ALL WERE ABLE TO TRAVEL THROUGH TIME LIKE THAT.

THAT STARLIGHT MUST BE PRETTY MAGICAL!

SHE OBVIOUSLY HAS MORE TALENT FOR MAGIC THAN ALMOST ANY PONY I'VE SEEN.

I WASN'T ABLE TO USE MY MAGIC TO STOP HER.

WELL, IF SHE'S AS POWERFUL AS ALL THAT, WE CAN'T JUST SEND HER ON HER WAY—

—CAN WE?

ACTUALLY, I KIND OF HAVE SOMETHING ELSE IN MIND.

OH, THEY'RE TAKING A LONG TIME!

WHUMP

YOU CAN COME IN NOW.

I KNOW THERE'S NO EXCUSE FOR WHAT I DID...

...BUT I'M READY FOR WHATEVER *PUNISHMENT* YOU THINK IS FAIR.

I'VE BEEN THINKING A LOT ABOUT HOW BADLY EQUESTRIA FARED WITHOUT JUST ONE GROUP OF FRIENDS.

BECAUSE WHEN EVEN ONE FRIENDSHIP DIES, THE RESULTS CAN BE DISASTROUS.

I KNOW, *FIRSTHOOF*, HOW TRUE THAT CAN BE.

AND THAT IS WHY I'VE ASKED YOU HERE.

IF YOU'RE WILLING TO LEARN, I'M WILLING TO TEACH YOU WHAT I KNOW.

YOU'LL HAVE THE POWER TO MAKE EQUESTRIA AN EVEN BETTER PLACE.

HOW DO I START?

STARTING IS *EASY*. ALL YOU HAVE TO DO IS MAKE A FRIEND.

AND YOU'VE GOT SEVEN OF THEM *RIGHT HERE*.

NOT THE END!